THE
HEART'S
CHOICE

ANNA MARKLAND

OLIVERHEBERBOOKS

Dedicated to the hardy folk of Lancashire.

Prologue

Bolton, Lancashire, England, 1862

Sergeant Halliwell tweaked one pointed tip of his handlebar mustache. "Remind me again, who discovered the body, Mr. Sandiford?" he asked.

Rising from the settee in the drawing room of his comfortable home, Roger clenched his jaw and wished he'd remained seated. At six feet in height, he was considered tall, but Halliwell dwarfed him. As Master of Broadclough Mill, Roger knew only too well how unsettling a death could be for the rest of the workforce, and the imposing sergeant struck him as a tenacious bulldog who'd wrestle with a mystery until he solved it. However, Roger had more pressing matters to deal with than the unfortunate death of one of his workers. "As I said, Miles Smethurst, my overseer, when he came to get the shift started."

"You keep asking the same question," Roger's mother declared, glaring at the policeman.

Lucinda Sandiford's impatient nature was well known, though perhaps not to this particular policeman from the Bolton Borough Constabulary. "The sergeant's just following procedure," Roger said, in an effort to appease his mother. "Although it does seem obvious what happened. Little piecers are often crushed by the spinning machines—a hazard of the job."

"Many little piecers are injured every year," Lucinda pointed out. "Crawling under the mechanized spinning looms to reattach broken cotton threads takes agility. Children don't always pay attention to what they are doing."

Roger bristled. He wasn't comfortable employing children to do such dangerous work, but adults were too big for the task. As a child, he'd worked as a piecer himself. He might be master of Broadclough Mill now, but he'd never forgotten the hardships of his youth. Piecers had to keep their wits about them, but they worked long hours and were often malnourished.

"The dead boy was known as a troublemaker," the sergeant replied.

"What does that have to do with it?" Lucinda asked.

"I've been told Smethurst had a run-in with Malcolm Pickering just yesterday."

"I'm not kept abreast of every problem that occurs in the mill," Roger replied. "I have an overseer to take care of that."

"But you personally have disciplined Pickering on previous occasions."

Prickly heat swept across Roger's nape. Something was very wrong. "Possibly, I have hundreds of employees. Why all the questions? I have a mill to run."

"I'm afraid the spinning room will have to remain out-of-bounds for the moment."

The knot in Roger's gut tightened. "Sergeant, you're perhaps not aware of the cotton famine currently threatening our industry. The American Civil War is starving us of cotton. We can't afford to lose a day's production. The workers' continued employment is hanging in the balance as it is."

He preferred not to mention the bleak outlook for his family and his business if the famine continued.

The policeman tucked his notebook into the pocket of his uniform and nestled the pencil stub behind his ear. "I am aware of the famine caused by the American Civil War," he replied in a patronizing manner. "But until we solve this murder, the spinning room is off limits."

"Murder?" Roger and his mother both exclaimed at once.

BACK AT POLICE HQ, Marcus Halliwell removed his stovepipe hat, stiffened his spine, and saluted the superior officer who'd assigned him to investigate the death at Broadclough Mill.

"Well?" the inspector asked from behind his desk. "Open and shut?"

"Murder, sir."

The inspector arched a doubtful brow. "You're certain? Children who work in the mills are often killed or injured."

"This lad's skull bore evidence of several sharp blows with something like a hammer. His body sustained no injuries, which I believe would have been the case had the machinery killed him."

The inspector frowned. "You must proceed with caution in this matter. We can't afford to get on the wrong side of the Sandifords, you know."

Marcus was tempted to make some remark about Mrs. Sandiford's abrasive manner but thought better of it. His inspector might be a friend of the Sandifords. Powerful people tended to stick together.

"Any suspects?"

At this point, Marcus had no idea who might be responsible, but this investigation was a chance to prove his capabilities. "I plan to interrogate the overseer and other mill workers. Malcolm Pickering was often in trouble with his supervisors."

"A pest they'd all sooner be rid of."

"Exactly, sir."

"Carry on, then. Just tread lightly with Sandiford. The mill owners are an influential lot."

Chapter 1

Good News And Bad

Milton Abbas, Dorset, England, 1862

Fearing she'd misheard, Beatrice Parker fought to extricate herself from the deep cushions of the settee. "A barony?" she exclaimed, eyes wide.

Her father drew on his pipe, filling the air with the redolent aroma of tobacco. "It would seem so, Bea," he replied, scanning the unexpected missive once again. "I didn't even know I had a distant cousin who was a baron. According to this letter, they've conducted an exhaustive search, and I'm Algernon Fothergill's only surviving relative."

"But where is this barony?" Bea's mother enquired.

"Somewhere in Lancashire," he answered. "Belmont Grange, near Bolton, apparently."

"It's out of the question," Abigail Parker retorted. "Lancashire is so … so…"

"Industrial," her husband supplied. "That's apparently true of the towns and cities. The birth of new industries and the decline of traditional ways of earning a living has resulted in thousands flocking to the towns. Improvements made to cope with the overcrowding are already inadequate. Cities and towns have been created such as the world has never seen before.

Great masses of people are living crammed close together. It's a new world, a new England."

"I've heard there are slums where the stench is unbearable," his wife murmured, clearly unimpressed by her husband's well-informed explanation.

"From what I've read," Bea's father added. "Muddy, rubbish-strewn alleys have become the norm in some places."

Arthur Parker was an avid reader who considered it his moral duty to keep up with current affairs, but Bea wondered where her mother had heard these rumors, since she rarely ventured out of the house. "Belmont Grange sounds rural," she said, struggling with conflicting emotions. *Rural* was certainly a word that described Milton Abbas, and she loved the quaint village where she'd lived for all of her nineteen years. However, life could be dull and predictable. Village folk had high expectations of the only child of the local vicar. She had just one friend her own age in Milton Abbas, and there were certainly no interesting young men. She and Edith enjoyed each other's friendship and weren't interested in pimply youths. The prospect of marriage to a farmer knotted her innards, whereas Edith Rexton had grown up on a farm and considered farming a fine life. When Bea accompanied her father on parochial visits to local farms, the stench of pigs and sheep churned her stomach.

"And, if I did consent to go, how would we travel such a great distance?" her mother asked.

Not consent to go? Bea deemed this a ridiculous notion. The Reverend Arthur Parker and his family barely survived on a diocesan pittance. Belmont Grange had an opulent ring to it. Surely her sickly mother wouldn't turn down an opportunity to live in comfort?

"I believe the train goes to Lancashire," her father replied.

"Not the train!" her mother exclaimed, clutching a lacy kerchief to her nose before she swooned.

"Glenda," her father shouted.

The family's maid-of-all-work bustled into the drawing room so quickly, Bea suspected she'd probably been listening at the door, as usual. With her came the overwhelming scent of her cheap *eau de toilette*. Glenda had worked for the Parkers since before Bea's birth and tended to think of herself as part of the family. "Oh, my poor mistress," she wailed, producing a small bottle of smelling salts from the deep pocket of her cotton apron. "Lancashire, of all places."

It was fortunate Bea's mother had been seated when she swooned. Glenda's large frame wasn't suited to kneeling, only eavesdropping.

Mrs. Parker's delicate constitution made her prone to fainting spells, hence the maid's readiness to address the latest episode.

"The train," Abigail moaned, as Glenda waved the uncorked bottle under her nose.

A good deal of sobbing and dire warnings about the horrors of train travel ensued as Bea and the maid helped her mother out of the armchair. After seeing her tucked into bed with Glenda repeating, *There, there*, over and over, Bea found her father at the desk in his cramped study.

"I'm replying to the lawyer in London," he explained. "Perhaps he can arrange our transportation to Belmont Grange. No harm in going to see the place."

Bea worried for her frail mother, but couldn't deny the excitement bubbling in her own heart. Moving north meant her father would have to give up his living. Once they made the trek, it was unlikely they'd ever come back. The prospect should have terrified her, but she found herself eager to set out.

~

WITH GLENDA'S HELP, they spent the next three weeks selling off bits and pieces of furniture and sundries. Some items, like the china cabinet and its contents, were difficult to part with. Her mother declared the whole enterprise too much to bear and took to her bed. They boxed up books which her father insisted on taking with him. Clothing and personal items lay ready to pack into valises. The parishioners organized a small but heart-felt send-off in the parish hall. She'd known them all since child-hood and felt guilty she wouldn't miss any of them, except her friend, Edith.

In the midst of this flurry of preparations, they received a surprise visitor. Abigail was delighted by her nephew's arrival from London. "How is my dear sister, Peter?" she asked over and over.

"She is well, Aunty," Bea's cousin replied. "What's this I hear about you moving north?"

Bea wondered how he knew of their changed circum-stances, but since her mother was clearly reluctant to explain, Bea told him, "Father has inherited a barony in Lancashire."

Peter winked at his uncle. "I suppose I'll have to address you as Baron Arthur," he jested.

"Nonsense, my boy. But you'll have to visit us once we're established in the north."

"Indeed I will," Peter replied. "Shall we take a walk in the grounds one last time, Beatrice?"

Tempted to make her excuses—she truly did have a lot to do —she couldn't ignore her mother's nod of approval. "Of course, Peter."

They strolled around the vicarage garden, until they came to her mother's favorite rambling rose. "I shall miss this," she confessed, inhaling the fragrance of the blossom he plucked from the arbor and presented to her. She was mortified when he suddenly dropped to one knee.

Casting aside the bloom, she urged him to stand. "Please, Peter. I do not wish to be rude, but ..."

He stood but took hold of her hands. "I realize this is a bad time, given your imminent move. However, I believe we are well suited. I'd be honored if ..."

"Please, Peter," she begged. "I am not ready to marry and I barely know you."

She didn't mention she'd never trusted him since a childhood visit to his mother's home in London. He'd pulled her hair and put a spider in her bed. Since his arrival, he'd struck her as an overconfident townie. Marrying such an irritating man was out of the question.

Peter departed Milton Abbas the same day, his nose clearly out of joint.

The next day, a Mr. James Odlum arrived unannounced. Bea's father greeted him like a long-lost son. Bea personally thought the young law clerk dispatched to Dorset by the late baron's solicitors had too high an opinion of himself. His superior tone was a sure sign he considered himself above their station, despite the fact Arthur Parker was now a baron. His frequent mention of an uncle who was a duke made it clear that escorting a parochial family to Lancashire was beneath his dignity. "But what's a young man to do when Messrs. Hardman, Burgesse, and Hilton instruct him to venture into the wilds of Dorset?" he asked. "After all, Messrs. Hardman, Burgesse, and Hilton have been the Baron's London solicitors forever."

Bea was mildly surprised this patronizing monologue didn't cause her mother to swoon, although Abigail Parker had managed to weather the startlingly foppish colors of the young man's attire and his cloying cologne without fainting.

Whenever she encountered the young man, Glenda seemed unable to take her eyes off his tight yellow pantaloons, pink ruffled shirt, and purple topcoat.

"Well, we appreciate your coming all this way to help us," Bea's affable father said. "We've never ventured further than Weymouth before."

"We'll start our journey from Poole," Odlum replied, in a tone that suggested Weymouth was beyond the pale. He then stuck his nose in the air and demanded Glenda show him to his chamber.

The Parkers had only ever referred to the guest room as *the back bedroom,* and Bea couldn't recall the last time it had housed a guest. She was quite certain Odlum wouldn't be happy with his cramped *chamber*.

Chapter 2

Vital Matters

Bolton, Lancashire, England

Roger Sandiford stroked the stubble on his chin with the backs of his fingers. Contemplating the dwindling supply of baled raw cotton on the receiving dock, he had to face the fact Broadclough Mills couldn't survive long at the current rate. Adding to the problem was the presence of a policeman investigating a murder at the mill. Sergeant Halliwell was of the opinion no spinning mule could have caved in Malcolm Pickering's skull. A hammer was more likely.

"Bluidy Peelers," his overseer exclaimed. "All this fuss over a dead brat."

"Pickering may have been a brat," Roger replied. "But we can't tolerate violence at the mill."

"They think I did it, tha knows."

"Did you?" Roger quipped.

"Nay. Pickering were a bad lad and I may have felt like killin' 'im many a time, but nay."

"Don't tell the police that."

"Already did. Halliwell made a note of it in his little book."

Roger gestured to the meager supply of raw cotton. "Meanwhile, we have more important matters to worry about."

"Bluidy Colonials," Miles agreed. "Their Civil War'll bring this business down if it ain't o'er soon."

Roger didn't always agree with Miles Smethurst, and he ought to point out America hadn't been a colony for almost a hundred years. However, in this case, his overseer was probably right. The profits from Roger's once-thriving mill had already plummeted. No cotton from America meant no work for his employees. Every mill in Lancashire was experiencing the same problem. Roger inhaled deeply, but the usual reek of dozens of sweaty working men laboring in the yard was missing. There were no shouts of friendly greetings or admonishment, no tang of oil in the air. Unemployment led to unrest, but he couldn't afford to keep the machines running without cotton to spin and weave.

"It's ironic," he told Miles. "We've weathered strikes, machine-breakers, even fire. Now, a war on the other side of the world and a murder threaten to close us down."

He didn't mention the years of struggle and sacrifice to get the mill up and running in the first place, nor the ruthless wheeling and dealing in which he'd had to involve himself. At twenty-five, he'd expected to be financially secure.

Miles nodded. "At least our workers support the fight agin slavery."

"There is that," Roger agreed. "Let's hope the anti-slavery spirit sustains them once the money runs out."

"On another subject, I 'ear there's to be a new occupant at Belmont Grange," Miles remarked.

"Aye, a vicar from a small village in Dorset, of all places. He'll find life in our northern county very different."

"This ain't the best o' times to be comin' north, I reckon," Miles said. "And they say the Grange needs a bit o' work."

It struck Roger somebody should perhaps have checked on the old house. He simply hadn't had time, and it was hardly his responsibility. "Well, the estate is five miles out of town and surrounded by moorland. Last time I was invited there, the place was looking jaded, and that's at least six years ago. They say Belmont went off his head shortly after that."

"Still, the old Baron, God rest him, kept his nose out o' thy business. I suppose gentry don't socialize wi' mill owners."

Roger shrugged. What did he care if members of the nobility looked down their noses at tradesmen? "Let's hope the same proves true for the new Baron Belmont."

Later the same afternoon, Roger attended the fortnightly meeting of local mill owners, held in the banquet room of *The Pack Horse* hotel. His frustration grew as *discussions* between his fellow mill owners degenerated into the usual squabbling. They had vital matters to resolve, yet the current argument centered on who amongst them should meet the new Baron when he arrived at Great Moor Street station in a few days. It was to be expected that a local businessman would put in an appearance.

"The chap from the London solicitors wrote to say he and the Baron's family will arrive on Thursday," Roderick Hampson shouted. "That's payday at my mill. I can't go."

Roger inhaled deeply and instantly regretted it. The mill owners in the small banquet room might be wealthy, but he'd warrant some of them hadn't bathed in a long while. Payday fell on the same day for every mill, but Hampson wasn't a man to tangle with. "I'll go," he yelled in exasperation, hoping they'd move on to discussing the famine.

"Are you allowed to leave Broadclough while the murder investigation is ongoing?" Hampson replied.

Curious frowns indicated most of those present hadn't

heard. Trust Hampson to mention it. "Why would it affect my movements? It's in hand. I'm confident the murderer will soon be apprehended."

Amid the ensuing shocked whispers, Hampson immediately brought down his gavel and adjourned the meeting. He announced refreshments were being served in the adjoining room, which meant there'd be copious amounts of ale consumed in the course of the afternoon.

Roger couldn't keep silent. "But aren't we going to discuss the American war and its effects on us? We initially believed the warehoused stocks would see out a brief conflict."

"Aye," Hampson retorted. "But all the early Union advances were driven back and it's becoming clear the war will drag on. Can't do nowt about it. Just have to lay people off till it's o'er."

A self-made man from a working-class family, Hampson was proud of his mode of speech. Yet, he had no empathy for the men, women and children he employed.

Roger had been born and brought up in a cellar dwelling in the maze of dark alleys near the Croal, a narrow, sluggish river that was more like a trickle of liquid filth than a waterway. He'd never forgotten the stench. When he was a child, cholera epidemics carried off many of their neighbors. In summer, his home swarmed with flies. He'd worked hard all his life and taken enormous risks to be where he was today. He knew what it was to go hungry, and was desperate for a better solution to the cotton famine. The nearby city of Manchester had formed a relief committee. Why couldn't Bolton do the same? Evidently, his fellow mill-owners didn't see the urgency.

Preferring not to spend his afternoon drinking watered ale, he left, emerging from the hotel into the busy street. He tossed a farthing to an urchin eager to clear a path with his broom through the ankle-deep mud and horse droppings. Bradshawgate was paved, but the endless stream of horse-drawn carriages made it impassable without the help of a sweeper. His attention was diverted by a band of minstrels who appeared oblivious to the filth and the traffic as they paraded down the middle of the busy street, singing and dancing for their supper.

He passed by most of the market stalls, ignoring the vendors of pickled whelks and pigs' trotters, trying to outshout each other. Feeling peckish, he stopped to purchase a meat pie from Mr. Thornley. The local butcher was one of the few who used real, lean beef in his pies, and the crust was always fresh.

"Tha's had a lad kilt," Thornley said, as he handed Roger his pie wrapped in greaseproof paper.

"Indeed," he replied, not really surprised by how quickly news had spread.

"Reckon that poor excuse fer a father did it," Thornley opined.

While it was true Joss Pickering was a belligerent drunkard, surely a man wouldn't kill his own son.

Chapter 3

Trains

"Will this nightmare soon be over?" Bea's mother asked, as Odlum herded the Parkers into their fourth dingy train compartment in two days, then rushed off to check that Glenda had made sure their luggage was loaded into the baggage car.

Bea herself was exhausted by guttural shouts of *All Change*, piercing whistles, slamming doors, garbled arrival and departure announcements, dark and dirty railway platforms, steam engines belching smoke, and choking air that blackened her nostrils. She'd never experienced jostling crowds before, nor been assailed by so many unidentifiable unpleasant odors. In Milton Abbas, people went about their business in a relaxed, easy-going manner. Everyone traveling by train seemed to be in a great hurry. However, excitement about a new adventure kept her going. In her opinion, trains were a wonderful invention, if noisy and dirty. The huge wheels of the engines were more than a little terrifying. She didn't share her opinions with her mother, who dreaded this new beginning and couldn't get over her conviction that locomotives were accidents waiting to happen. At least she hadn't swooned.

The train stopped at every little station between Poole and Waterloo Station. This made the journey seem never-ending, but the scenery was pleasing, until they reached the outskirts of London.

They lodged at the Hotel Victoria after a chaotic journey through London traffic from Waterloo Station to Euston Station. Glenda had a loud confrontation with the porter who showed them to their rooms. Odlum chided her behavior, calling her a country bumpkin, though he was the one every passerby stared at. She remained tight-lipped and sulky after his tirade. Odlum himself spent the night in the hotel on the opposite side of the Euston Arch because it "catered to a better class of person."

After their stay at the less-than-salubrious Hotel Victoria, they boarded a train for Manchester. As they traveled north, the landscape changed. Long stretches of open fields and majestic oaks and beeches reminded Bea of Dorset, but the increasingly large towns consisted of grime-encrusted buildings, factory chimneys belching smoke, and row upon row of terraced houses crammed together.

Bea's parents dozed for hours during most of the interminable way north. Glenda snored. Odlum was nowhere to be seen in the crowded third-class carriage. In fact, as soon as they were settled in this last train from Manchester to Bolton, she was certain he'd bolt for first class after checking on the baggage.

"Last lap," she said, in response to her mother's question. "Bolton next stop."

"Thank goodness James came with us," her father said wearily. "He's been a godsend."

Bea privately thought the fop should invest in more than one pair of pantaloons, perhaps in more sober colors and less tight-fitting.

~

Having arrived in good time, Roger paced the forecourt of Great Moor Street station. He checked his pocket watch numerous times, willing the Parkers' train to arrive at the empty platform each time he passed by the gate. The railway had made the transportation of goods easier for businessmen like himself, but was it too much to ask that passenger trains keep to the scheduled arrival times? He made it a point to always be punctual, more often than not arriving early for an appointment.

Aware the Belmont estate possessed only one dilapidated carriage, he'd brought his own brougham. The new Baron Belmont would find out soon enough that the estate had been neglected for many years.

Earlier in the day, he'd spoken with Pickering's father. It wasn't surprising Malcolm was such a tearaway. His father was a brute who often came to work inebriated. The fellow had turned up for his shift, even though the spinning room was still closed, three days after the incident. "Better'n bein' 'ome wi' the missus," he'd insisted.

Roger thought to reply that the grieving mother probably needed comforting, but he doubted Pickering gave a fig for his wife's feelings. He hardly seemed bothered by the fact his son had been murdered, and evidently preferred loitering idly at the mill to staying home with Mrs. Pickering.

Roger's patience was wearing thin when the great iron horse snorted and chugged into the station, plumes of black smoke adding to the grime on the glass panels in the vaulted platform canopy. Jolted from his reverie about the murdered boy's father, Roger walked toward the platform gate.

No sooner had the wheels squealed to a halt when a young man stepped down from the first-class carriage. "City ponce," Roger muttered, curious as to why the fellow clad in bright yellow trousers was heading away from the gate. Clouds of steam obscured the platform for several minutes. Out of the mist came the fop, accompanied by a motley crew. The older couple were much as Roger expected. The stunningly beautiful redhead supporting her mother was not. She was soberly dressed, but his male body reacted predictably to the generous swell of her breasts and shapely hips.

A portly maidservant trudged in the family's wake, a large valise in each pudgy hand, a portmanteau tucked under her arm.

As soon as they were through the gate, Roger stepped forward to introduce himself to the new Baron Belmont.

The fop came between them. "Be a good chap and assist the menial so she can make sure the luggage gets unloaded."

BEA GASPED. Odlum considered himself a sophisticated man-about-town, yet he'd mistaken the tall, well-dressed gentleman for a servant.

"I am not a porter, sir," the man replied, elbowing Odlum aside as he offered a hand to Bea's father and removed his top hat. "My name is Roger Sandiford, master of Broadclough Mills. The local business community bids you and your family welcome, my lord."

Disappointment flooded Bea. She'd felt an instant attraction to the handsome fellow, but he was a tradesman, not a gentleman after all. He'd barely been able to utter the words, *my lord*, as if they stuck in his throat.

"Good of you to meet us, Sandiford," Bea's father replied, as they shook hands.

"My task here is complete," Odlum declared. "This *businessman* can take care of conveying you to Belmont Grange."

Bea understood the snarl that marred Sandiford's chiseled features when Odlum hissed the word *businessman* and eyed him with disdain.

"Indeed," Sandiford replied, dark eyes narrowed at the yellow pantaloons. "You can run along."

Odlum hesitated, apparently not quite grasping that he'd been summarily dismissed. Bea's father put him out of his misery by shaking his hand and thanking him profusely, whereupon he strutted off.

Bea was glad to see him go but wasn't sure how to greet Sandiford. Her limited social circle in Dorset didn't include mill-owners, or men at all for that matter.

"Arthur Parker," her father said, saving the day. "May I introduce my wife, Abigail, and my daughter, Beatrice."

Sandiford might not be a gentleman, but he knew enough to bestow a courtly kiss on her mother's knuckles. "Baroness," he said politely.

Bea was strangely disappointed when he merely nodded in her general direction and muttered, "Miss Parker," as he settled the shiny top hat back on his black locks.

Chapter 4

Belmont Grange

It was unfortunate that Roger's driver had no choice but to take them through one of the seediest areas of Bolton when they left Great Moor Street station in the brougham. The cobblestone streets made for a bumpy ride.

Glenda and most of the luggage had to be left behind. The surly maid seemed unimpressed by Roger's promise to send a wagon.

Mrs. Parker was visibly impressed by the quality of his carriage, but she looked frail and worn out, which was understandable given the distance they'd traveled. Eyes closed and kerchief held firmly to her nose once the carriage was in motion, she might have dozed off for all Roger could tell.

Arthur Parker kept up a steady stream of conversation, asking about the town and Roger's mill.

Miss Parker didn't utter a word, but her deep frown clearly showed her dismay as they passed slums and derelict buildings. Garrulous women plucked chickens in the street. Empty crates littered the pavement. Grubby, unshaven men loitered outside *The Wheatsheaf*, waiting for opening time.

She cringed when his driver shouted obscenities at the horde of ragged children chasing the carriage, begging for money. He'd noticed her disdain when he introduced himself as a mill-owner. Obviously, a tradesman wasn't considered the social equal of a baron's daughter.

He foresaw difficulties ahead for the haughty Miss Parker if she thought life in Lancashire was going to be the same as the one she'd left behind in the south.

"As it happens," he told Parker. "Our route takes us by my mill. This is Broadclough coming up on the left."

Normally a hive of activity, before the American Civil War brought about the cotton famine, today the mill boasted an almost empty loading dock and idle laborers hanging about. Thankfully, Sergeant Halliwell was nowhere to be seen. Roger ordered the driver to stop, then beckoned Billy Wiggins. "There's a servant named Glenda waiting at Great Moor Street with luggage," he told the spinners' gaffer. "Send a man with a wagon and tell him to fetch her to the Grange."

Unwilling to launch into an explanation for the lack of activity as they resumed the journey, he instead told the Parkers, "I'm relieved none of the men were smoking, otherwise I'd have been forced to remonstrate with them."

"I suppose fire can be a problem," Parker replied. "All that cotton."

"Fire is the biggest danger any mill faces. More than one establishment in Lancashire has gone up in smoke with heavy loss of life when workers were trapped."

While he spoke true, he couldn't help but think fire hadn't been the cause of Malcolm Pickering's death. Satisfied they'd passed his mill without his having to confess to these strangers that things weren't going well, he wasn't prepared for the horror in Miss Parker's wide eyes. It was as well he hadn't mentioned the murder. A man could drown in those green depths.

∽

BEA COULDN'T RID herself of the horrific image of people burning alive inside a fire-ravaged factory. Cobblestones soon gave way to streets paved with what Sandiford told her father was a mixture of flint and grit. The carriage wheels threw up a fine dust.

"We're lucky it's not raining," Sandiford remarked.

Unwilling to contemplate the significance of his remark, she relaxed a little when the dirty streets of the town gave way to moorland. It wasn't the picturesque landscape of Dorset's downs, but the air was easier to breathe and there were no ragged beggars. Her mother rallied briefly, but lapsed back into sleep after a quick glance out of the window.

Bea didn't know what to think about Broadclough Mills. Roger Sandiford might be considered a handsome man if one were impressed by brooding good looks, or by the way his black hair curled into his nape. His intelligent brown eyes were disturbingly dark. His black topcoat and trousers were well tailored, his winged collar starched, his neckcloth tied perfectly. The brougham was a splendid vehicle which spoke of financial success. However, there didn't seem to be much going on at the mill itself.

They were obliged to stop two or three times to wait for moorland sheep to wander out of the way. A few skeletal trees clung to rocky outcroppings. A knot of dread tightened in Bea's stomach when the rolling moorland with the occasional patch of purple heather soon turned into a barren, windswept plateau.

Her fears were confirmed when Belmont Grange came into view. She said a silent prayer of thanks that her mother was still asleep and hoped she remained so until Glenda arrived with the smelling salts.

~

ROGER WASN'T surprised when the state of Belmont Grange shocked even the chatty Arthur Parker into silence.

The decrepit mansion stood as a haunting reminder of its former glory, shrouded in a wild tapestry of nature reclaiming its territory. The once-grand structure was now draped in thick vines and ivy, with trees whose roots had begun to intertwine with the foundation. Cracked stone walls were coated by layers of grime and moss.

The overgrown gardens were a chaotic blend of wild-flowers and towering weeds. Nature had taken over the mani-cured hedges and pathways. Trees unsuited to a moorland landscape had withered for lack of care. They loomed like sentinels, their gnarled branches casting eerie shadows. Amidst the tangled underbrush, the head of a moss-covered statue poked out here and there. A crumbling fountain in front of the house hadn't seen water in years. Pathways meandered into the unknown.

The house belonged in one of Mrs. Radcliffe's Gothic novels, yet it held an intriguing charm. "Belmont Grange has a rich history," he told the gaping threesome. A mischievous need to lighten the mood took hold of his tongue. "Are you brave enough to venture inside to uncover this house's mysteries?"

~

TEARS TRICKLED down Abigail Parker's cheeks when she startled awake and looked at her new home. Bea decided it was up to her to do what she could to soften the blow for her parents. They weren't elderly by any measure, but neither were they in the first flush of youth. Abigail in particular would have a difficult time dealing with this travesty. She rose to Sandiford's cheeky challenge. "We are indeed brave enough. Would you please summon the servants to assist us?"

"I'm afraid Algernon sent them all away. He grew rather paranoid in his dotage. Thought they were trying to poison him." He leaned closer to Bea's ear. "I suspect it was more a case of no funds to pay wages."

He had come inappropriately close, but his warm breath tickling her ear wasn't unpleasant. However, if her first sight of the house wasn't enough to confirm the estate was in financial difficulty, Sandiford's aside was the last nail in the coffin of her hopes. Her parents had a little money set aside from the sale of furniture, but not nearly enough to put this place to rights. "Come along," she urged, linking arms with them both after Mr. Sandiford helped them alight. "We'll soon have this house fixed up."

Bea filled her lungs as Sandiford put a broad shoulder to the reluctant door, then the trio followed him into the dark foyer. She half closed her eyes, suspecting there was nothing good to see. As if sensing they shouldn't linger, he led the way into what she supposed had once served as a sitting room.

Towering windows, many cracked or obscured by foliage, allowed slivers of light to filter into the dim interior, casting ghostly shadows that danced across dusty wooden floors. The odors of rodent droppings, mildew, and decay mingled with the faint hint of something vaguely floral.

The room held remnants of lives once lived there, with faded photographs and tattered curtains rustling gently in an invisible breeze, whispering secrets of the past.

Her mother sank into a settee, unleashing a cloud of dust that brought on a coughing fit. "I can go no further," she croaked.

Bea was surprised she'd managed to remain upright for as long as she had.

"I'll stay with Mother," her father said.

Exiting the room, Bea and Sandiford made their way to the central staircase. The threadbare carpet on the creaking stairs spoke of bygone wealth. The landing led to a darkened hallway lined with doors that squealed ominously when coaxed open. The remnants of opulent furnishings lay beneath layers of dust. "This place has known elegance and luxury," she whispered.

She hadn't meant the remark to be overheard, but Sandiford nodded. "Aye, it has."

His rich baritone chased away the chill, but she clutched his arm and shrieked when a mouse ran across her path. He put his arm around her waist and supported her until she calmed. "My apologies," she murmured, mortified she'd touched him, though his strength had warmed her. "Thank goodness you were with me. I went cold all over."

"Indeed," he agreed, rubbing her arms. "A cat might be a good idea, but I'll send out the rat catcher."

"Do you think there are rats?" she asked nervously.

"Probably not, but I'll protect you if any dare to appear. Are you able to carry on with the tour?"

She took comfort in Roger Sandiford's offer of protection and his teasing smile.

Downstairs once more, they investigated the dining room. A long table with two dozen or so mismatched chairs hinted at joyous gatherings now lost to history.

The ruined house served as a poignant reminder of the precarious nature of life. Every corner held a story waiting to be discovered.

But there were practicalities to face before Bea could indulge in fanciful thoughts of investigating the house's history. "Obviously, we cannot stay here until the place has been thoroughly cleaned," she told Sandiford.

"I apologize," he said. "I haven't been here in some time. Had I realized ..."

She privately thought a person charged with welcoming them would have made a better job of making sure the house was ready to receive them. "Yes," she said. "If you could recommend a nearby hotel."

Chapter 5

Stay With Us

Guilt plagued Roger. Rumor had it the Grange was in a derelict state, yet he'd been too preoccupied with the famine and the murder to consider the welfare of the new baron and his family. He had no time for the nobility who looked down their noses at people like him who'd made their fortunes in industry.

He'd never considered he might take a liking to the Parkers, nor that their beautiful and intelligent daughter would rouse potent male urges.

"I won't hear of it," he replied, suspecting the expense of a good hotel was something the Parkers couldn't afford. "My home is more comfortable than any hotel in this vicinity. I insist you stay with us. I'll also hire a crew to put the house to rights."

"Thank you, sir," Mrs. Parker sighed with relief.

"Er ..." Arthur said.

"The Businessmen's Association will gladly foot the bill," Roger lied, willing to absorb an expense that had resulted from his lack of interest in the arrival of a new occupant. He could only hope the newcomers wouldn't get wind of the murder while staying under his roof.

He assisted the Parkers to board the carriage, taking ludicrous pleasure in inhaling a whiff of Miss Parker's perfume. Lavender, if he wasn't mistaken. He chided himself. Since when had he cared about a woman's perfume? Still, the subtle aroma filled his nostrils as they made their way back to the town, adding to the discomfort of the stubborn swelling at his groin.

BEATRICE HAD NEVER SPENT so much time at close quarters with a man. She assumed that was the reason she felt—well, truth be told, she didn't know how to describe her feelings.

Strange, wanton cravings assailed her, which was scandalous. She wanted to trace a finger down Sandiford's long sideburns, then touch his proud chin. He was an attractive man, but he was a tradesman who hadn't taken the time to make sure their derelict house was made ready. As the daughter of a baron, she now had a position to uphold in the local community.

And what did he mean? *Stay with us.* Did he have a wife? The possibility left her strangely bereft.

An errant thought occurred. "Poor Glenda," she exclaimed.

Sandiford patted her hand. "Don't worry, Beatrice. I'll send word."

She should have been affronted. He'd touched her, and she hadn't given him leave to use her given name. Instead, she stifled the urge to let her hand creep into the safekeeping of his long fingers with their clean fingernails.

"I apologize," he said, clamping both hands on powerful thighs. "That was forward of me, Miss Parker. I had hoped we might become friends."

Friends? With a man? The notion was absurd. "I'd like that," she cooed, fluttering eyelashes she'd evidently lost control of.

ROGER RARELY FELT FLUMMOXED, but he found it hard to believe Miss Parker was flirting with him. Or had something in her eye caused the odd fluttering of eyelashes? She'd meshed her fingers together and seemed annoyed with herself, so obviously, she wasn't a practiced flirt.

He wondered what his widowed mother would think of her? Lucinda Sandiford had a well-deserved reputation in the local community as a tyrant. She'd supported him every step of the way from slum tenants to mill owners, often sacrificing her own needs to further his ambitions. Indeed, he doubted he would have fulfilled his dreams had it not been for his mother's iron will.

Now, the cotton famine threatened the mill's very existence, and the murder would further complicate matters.

Perhaps he'd been hasty offering his home as a temporary residence. Lucinda despised weakness, and she considered the American Civil War as a weakness that was wreaking havoc on the world at large. Roger suspected she resented her own inability to do anything about the situation. She wouldn't have much patience with the frail Mrs. Parker. He'd inherited his mother's disdain for the nobility, so the Parkers couldn't expect her respect unless they earned it. It was doubtful she'd remain silent on the topic of the police investigation.

As for his younger sister, he'd never understood the reason Philippa had always escaped the sting of their mother's rigid discipline. Compared to Miss Beatrice Parker, Philippa was ...

He shook his head. What kind of man compared his own flesh and blood to a woman he'd just met? "Here we are," he said, as the brougham entered the courtyard of his home.

Miss Parker frowned. "Your home is next door to the mill?" she asked, her imperious tone making it obvious she wrongly assumed Sandiford Manor would be lacking amenities.

He sighed. Lucinda would take an instant dislike to Miss Parker. Philippa would feel it necessary to belittle a woman who was clearly more refined than she.

Roger nodded. "Unlike many who abandoned their large houses and moved away from the industrial areas, we decided to stay. We didn't want our home turned into a squalid tenement, which is what has happened to most of them. I've heard tales of large families living in one room."

"Admirable," Parker exclaimed. "This way you can keep a close eye on your investment. I hope there'll be an opportunity to tour the mill while we are lodging here."

"Certainly," Roger replied, wondering how he'd explain the idle spinning room. But he chuckled inwardly. Lucinda might actually take a liking to Arthur Parker, baron or no.

Beatrice feared her father had taken leave of his senses. Tour the mill? She'd read about working conditions in mills. Noisy machinery, cotton floating in the air like snow. Men, women, and children who worked from dawn till dusk. She would not be accompanying her father if he insisted on touring the mill.

Her mother apparently also thought the notion too much to bear. She chose the moment to mutter, "Oh, dear," and swoon into Mr. Sandiford's arms as he helped her alight. He scooped her up as if she weighed nothing at all.

Bea was suddenly consumed by a ridiculously jealous urge to be carried in Roger Sandiford's strong arms. However, she wasn't prone to fainting, and he was no country bumpkin. He'd easily discern her malady as a ploy. And what would she hope to achieve with such a trick? He was not a gentleman. They might become friends, though never firm friends. Certainly not lovers. She suddenly felt overheated. Where on earth had that unladylike thought come from?

As they approached the house's portico, Sandiford shouted to a man loitering beside the nearby loading dock. "Has Wiggins sent the wagon yet to pick up the luggage?"

The worker seemed taken by surprise. Coughing, he quickly hid something behind his back. "Aye, Mr. Sandiford," he replied hoarsely.

Bea gasped as she witnessed an unbelievable transformation in Sandiford's handsome features. He promptly handed her mother over to her husband and stalked off toward the worker.

Arthur staggered under the unexpected weight.

Bea feared she truly might faint. She'd never want to be the object of the anger that reddened Sandiford's face and contorted his beguiling smile into a grimace.

Chapter 6

Mrs. Sandiford

Roger regretted having to deal with John Smythe in front of the Parkers, but if his mother had seen the man smoking from her window, he'd have been dealt with in a far worse manner. He seized the tattered lapels of Smythe's jacket and shoved him against the dock. "Put it out," he growled.

"It's out," Smythe replied, resentment blazing in his eyes.

"Throw it down," Roger insisted, lifting the idiot off his feet. "Let me see."

The still glowing butt fell to the ground where Roger stomped on it. "You're sacked," he shouted, punching the man squarely in the jaw. "Get off the property."

Smythe dropped to his knees. "Sorry, Master," he pleaded, fear in his eyes now. "My children will starve if I don't work."

"You should have thought of that before you risked the mill and your fellow workers. Your own children work for me; do you want them burned alive?"

"Ain't no work anyways," Smythe hissed, as Roger shoved him out the mill gate.

"And don't come back," he yelled, dismayed by the horror on the faces of Arthur Parker and his daughter when he turned.

"They never learn," he growled, taking up the burden of Mrs. Parker once more. "I'll not tolerate smoking on mill property and they know it."

BEA's original opinion was confirmed. Sandiford definitely was not a gentleman. He was, in fact, a bully, a brawler, a man who used his fists to solve problems. Surely there was no need to render a worker and his family destitute simply because he'd smoked one of those nasty cigarettes.

Yet, he took her mother back into his arms with great care. "He's a contradiction, for sure," she muttered to herself.

On the outside, Sandiford's two-story home appeared to be part of the mill. Closer inspection revealed it to be a separate building. Large, mullioned windows overlooked the mill yard. Made of local stone, it looked solid and substantial. Stepping inside the front door, held open by a liveried footman, Bea discovered the Sandiford family lived in very opulent surroundings. Despite the lack of activity at the mill, he must be wealthy. Of course, it was wealth built on the backs of the working class. In Dorset, there'd always been a divide between rich and poor, but there'd also been families like her own who weren't poor, simply not well-off. And everyone respected everyone else, despite the differences in their stations. From what she'd seen of Lancashire, there seemed to be only two classes, the masters and the workers. So far, she'd seen only animosity between the two. She wondered how the late Baron Belmont had fit into this structure. And how would she and her family fare in this very industrial setting?

It seemed the baron had isolated himself out on the moor. She couldn't imagine her father accepting such a role. Nor did she wish to live in isolation amid bleak surroundings. She'd always taken an active role in her father's good works in Milton Abbas, and wanted to be part of this society that was so very different from all she knew. She sensed that here in Bolton, there was an even greater need for good works. Perhaps she'd have to pluck up her courage and accompany her father if he did take a tour of the mill.

Before disappearing up a flight of carpeted stairs with his burden, their host gave clipped commands to a butler who took their hats and gloves. Traversing the highly polished tiles of the foyer, Bea glimpsed several tasteful Greek statues and elegant floral arrangements before she and her father were led into an enormous drawing room.

A sour-faced older lady dressed in a high-necked frock of black bombazine rose quickly from an upholstered Georgian settee. "Who are you people?" she demanded to know.

"Yer pardon, er ... Mrs. Sandiford," the butler stammered, clearly intimidated by his mistress. "Baron ... er..."

"You're the new baron?" Mrs. Sandiford asked, eyes narrowed. "That's all we need."

Bea was left in no doubt that the unfriendly woman who eyed them up and down had found them wanting.

WHEN ROGER RETURNED from depositing Mrs. Parker in a guest bedroom in the capable hands of a maidservant, the grim expression on his mother's face left little doubt she was annoyed. For a woman who'd endured untold hardships, Lucinda seemed to grow increasingly short-tempered with age. "Good, Mama," he declared, in an effort to smooth her ruffled feathers. "You've met Arthur Parker, Baron Belmont, and his daughter, Beatrice."

"I have," she replied sarcastically.

"May I introduce my mother, Lucinda Sandiford."

"My honor, ma'am," Parker said, as he bowed. Miss Parker bobbed a polite curtsey.

Still, his mother's stern demeanor didn't relax.

He invited the Parkers to be seated. "The Grange is in deplorable condition," he explained to his mother. "Not fit to live in, so I invited our newcomers to stay here until I can get the house livable."

"There is no Mrs. Parker?" Lucinda asked.

"The journey took a toll on my mother," Miss Parker replied.

"I've left her in a guest room with Polly," Roger added.

"I suppose you had no alternative but to bring them here," his mother said. "But it isn't a good time, as you well know."

Lucinda had never been one for social niceties, but Roger wished she'd at least try to make the Parkers welcome. He didn't want Beatrice to think all northerners were Neanderthals. His earlier fisticuffs had probably left that impression in her mind, and when she heard about the murder ...

He was mildly annoyed that he even wanted her good opinion. She and her family would eventually move out to the moor and he'd likely see very little of her.

The prospect was keenly disappointing.

As THE ONLY vicar in Milton Abbas and the surrounding area, Arthur Parker had always been greeted with respect wherever he went. The family might not be wealthy, but they considered themselves genteel.

Mrs. Sandiford's unfriendly reception shocked Beatrice and left her in no doubt that the structure of society was very different here in the north. Mrs. Sandiford maintained her stern demeanor even after being informed she was speaking with a baron. Clearly, noble titles meant nothing to the woman. Nor did she welcome this intrusion into her home.

To his credit, Roger Sandiford did his best to keep a conversation going. Uncharacteristically hesitant, Bea's father supplied stilted replies. Mrs. Sandiford sat as stiff as a ramrod. There was no offer of tea.

After ten uncomfortable minutes that seemed more like half an hour, the butler was summoned and instructed to lead Bea and her father to the guest suites. They took their leave and followed the butler.

"Let's hope it doesn't take long to ready the Grange," she whispered, when they were left alone in a pleasant sitting room between the two suites.

"Yes, Mrs. Sandiford isn't a happy woman," her father replied. "Do you get the feeling there's something they're not telling us?"

His insight and his query gave Bea pause. She'd simply assumed the woman was unfriendly, but there could be more to it.

~

"THE GIRL HAS her eye on you," Roger's mother told him after their guests left the drawing room.

"Nonsense," he replied. "We're from two different worlds."

"Mark me well," Lucinda insisted. "I saw the way she looks at you."

"She doesn't even like me," he retorted. "And I'm not sure I like her."

"Now you're talking rubbish. I know when a man is interested in a woman."

Roger acknowledged he'd never win the argument, and in

truth, he *was* attracted to Beatrice Parker. His mother knew him too well. "We should be more concerned with this cotton famine and the murder. We'll have to take drastic measures soon. I assume worrying about that is the reason you were so unfriendly to our guests."

"Borden tells me we have house guests," his sister declared, as she swooped into the room.

"The new Baron Belmont and his family," Lucinda explained. "The Grange is apparently a ruin."

"Well, they can't stay here," Philippa declared.

"It's temporary until the house can be made ready," Roger replied, weary of his sister's temperamental outbursts.

Philippa pouted. "But I've invited my friends to stay for a house party. It's bad enough we have policemen crawling all over the mill."

The hackles rose on Roger's nape. There was one policeman on the case, and the tall, well-muscled Halliwell certainly wasn't a man who crawled. "Sister, dear, you're obviously unaware the mill is in dire straits. You must cut down on these frivolities. Is that another new frock I've paid for?"

Philippa glowered. "So, I'm expected to live like a nun simply because you can't make the mill pay?"

Roger fisted his hands, angry that his mother tolerated this nonsense from her daughter and didn't come to his defense. "Let me explain the situation in terms you might understand. The Americans are fighting a civil war. There is no cotton coming from there. Our cotton mill depends on a steady supply. Do you see?"

"Pooh," his sister exclaimed. "I'm sure the other mill owners have found alternative sources of cotton, and I'll warrant they don't have dead bodies littering up their spinning rooms."

With that, she turned abruptly and flounced out.

"And cancel the house party," he yelled at the door.

"You're too hard on her," his mother said.

"Then you speak to her," he retorted. "She might listen to you."

Chapter 7

Fine Dining

The next morning, Roger had no choice but to offer his study to Sergeant Halliwell when the policeman requested a secure, private place to conduct interviews. It appeared those in command of the Bolton Borough Police hadn't deemed this a serious enough case to send a detective to investigate.

Roger couldn't think of any reason for the Parkers to visit his study, and the policeman would at least be tucked out of the way if his guests happened to wander about the house.

He was taken aback when Halliwell asked him to be present while he questioned Joss Pickering. "I'd appreciate your opinion," the sergeant said.

"Do you suspect the father of murdering his own son?" Roger asked.

"At the moment, I suspect everybody. Rumor has it Pickering's a violent man."

Roger privately thought rumor wasn't a sound basis for convicting a man of murder, but he wasn't a policeman and hoped *everybody* didn't include him as a suspect.

Halliwell positioned himself in the leather chair behind the desk. Roger sat in one of the upholstered chairs by the hearth so he could study the profile of the person being questioned.

Pickering dithered when he entered the study. With him came the unpleasant odor of a man clad in clothes he's worn for a very long time, and the unmistakable reek of liquor.

Roger understood the man's hesitation. The study was an imposing room, especially for a cotton spinner who probably lived in a hovel, and who'd likely never cracked open a book. The walls were lined with shelves crammed full of leather-bound learned tomes. Only Roger and his mother knew they'd been purchased as a job lot from an estate sale. He preferred to read Dickens. Lucinda enjoyed the adventures of Black Bess, Sweeney Todd, and their ilk. As for Philippa, spending money on the latest fashions was her favorite pastime.

"Be seated, Mr. Pickering," Halliwell commanded, nodding to the chair in front of the desk. "And take off your cap."

Pickering rushed to obey and sat with cloth cap in hand.

"Did you kill your son?" Halliwell asked bluntly.

When Pickering opened his mouth to reply, Halliwell cringed.

Roger would wager a spark might set the man's breath alight, but he caught the flash of outrage before Pickering controlled it.

"I'll be 'onest, there's bin times I wanted to wring 'is neck, but I couldn't kill me own flesh and blood."

"When did you last see Malcolm?"

Pickering licked his lips, no doubt wishing he had a drink in his hand. "Yesterday, outside yon mill after t' shift."

"Did you walk home together?"

Studying his cap, Pickering whispered his response.

"Louder, please."

"I stopped off at *T' Three Crowns* afore I went 'ome."

"And how long where you there?"

"Till closin' time. Landlord'll vouch fer me."

"No doubt," Halliwell replied, with more than a hint of disgust. "So, you have no idea if Malcolm went home?"

"Tha'll 'ave to ask 'is mam."

Halliwell sighed, looked across at Roger, then dismissed Pickering, who replaced his cap and shuffled out.

"What do you think?" the sergeant asked.

"Well, if the innkeeper backs up his alibi, I'd say he's innocent. He's a drunk, but a murderer?"

"Aye, I think you're right. I'll pay Mrs. Pickering a visit."

Marcus Halliwell was worried when he left Sandiford's study. He'd been sure Joss Pickering would turn out to be the killer, but now he had doubts. Perhaps it was just as well. A man murdering his own son didn't bear thinking about. It was no wonder a boy went off the rails when he had a father who spent more time in the alehouse than at home.

However, the investigation was back to square one. He had no credible suspects. The plan to interview Mrs. Pickering was perhaps a waste of time. Obviously, Malcolm hadn't gone home after his shift in the mill.

The overseer was the prime suspect now. He had motive—Pickering was a thorn in his side. He *found* the body—too convenient perhaps. A man responsible for the smooth running of a cotton mill must own a hammer.

Heading for the foyer, he was about to nestle his stovepipe back on his head when a young woman crossed his path. She hesitated when she saw him. He didn't recognize her, but thought she might be the new Baron Belmont's daughter Mr. Sandiford had spoken of. "Miss," he said politely before continuing out of the house.

THE FIRST EVENING at Sandiford Manor, Bea was nervous about dining with the family but had to admit they set a fine table. The china was Crown Derby, the cutlery Sheffield stainless steel, the wine and water glasses lead crystal. The startlingly white tablecloth and napkins were woven damask, the enormous chandelier hanging overhead also lead crystal. A heady aroma wafted from an enormous bouquet of lilies in the center of the table.

Liveried footmen served the five-course meal and poured the wine with practiced ease and decorum.

"The braised lamb is from a local flock," Sandiford told his guests.

"It's delicious," Bea replied honestly. "You must have a good cook."

"Why wouldn't we?" the mill owner's sister retorted.

Bea didn't know what to make of Philippa Sandiford. She at least smiled, which was more than could be said for her mother, but the smile didn't reach her eyes. There was palpable tension between brother and sister, who glared at each other across the table.

"Miss Parker is simply being polite," Sandiford said, his voice tinged with irritation. "It takes a good cook to produce such a dish, and we have a fine one in Martha."

"I suppose we'll have to let her go in the circumstances," Philippa declared spitefully.

Roger gritted his teeth.

Mrs. Sandiford bristled. "That's quite enough, Philippa dear," she said, in a chillingly calm tone of voice.

Bea was perplexed. Good cooks were hard to find. Why would they let theirs go? What circumstances? There was an undercurrent to the conversation she couldn't put her finger on.

Did it have something to do with the policeman she'd seen exiting one of the downstairs rooms earlier in the day?

"Glenda has cooked most of our meals since I was born," she explained, in an effort to banish the silence. "But nothing as delicious as this."

"Speaking of Glenda," Bea's father said. "I hope it's not too inconvenient to let her stay here."

"Not at all," Sandiford replied. "The servants' quarters are spacious. No doubt she's already been directed to a vacant bedroom."

"She'll spend most of her time caring for my mother," Bea said.

Sandiford nodded. "I'm sorry Mrs. Parker wasn't well enough to join us this evening."

Mrs. Sandiford snorted.

Bea thought it best not to let her irritation show. Mrs. Sandiford clearly enjoyed ruffling feathers. "It was good of you to send a tray up for her," she replied, bestowing a grateful smile on her host.

"Perhaps she'll feel better tomorrow," he said politely.

Bea doubted her frail mother would ever fully recover from this move to Lancashire. Yet, here they were in a more luxurious house than any in Milton Abbas. The Sandifords might not be gentry, but the Parkers could be sitting in the splendid house of a local nobleman.

When they returned to their private sitting room, Bea shared her thoughts with her father. "In days gone by, I suppose the aristocrats were the moneyed families. Now, the wealthy industrialists are the new aristocrats."

"Very observant of you, my dear," he replied. "However, for generations, dukes and earls have inherited money and estates. With that came privilege. Men like Roger Sandiford have had to work for what they have. That doesn't make them lesser men."

After dropping in to check on her sleeping mother for a few minutes, Bea retired, her thoughts full of her father's wisdom. Arthur Parker saw Sandiford as a worthy man. It was confusing. How did she view Roger Sandiford? The snob in her found him lacking, but he drew her like a lodestone. Yes, that was it. Magnetic.

~

ROGER'S MOTHER glared pointedly at his restless fingers drumming the table, but he didn't stop. Conflicting emotions coursed through his veins. No matter the opulent surroundings in which they lived, the members of his family seemed to have little idea of how to behave civilly.

Philippa's spendthrift ways threatened to make a bad situation worse. Both she and his mother had behaved rudely. The Sandifords weren't aristocrats, and he had no desire to belong to the upper class, but could his mother and sister not cease behaving as if they still lived in the slums?

Despite Arthur Parker's elevation to a barony, the family wasn't upper class and didn't deserve to be treated rudely. His increasing desire to get closer to Beatrice seemed more out of reach than ever.

"If you want to marry well," his mother told Philippa, "You must learn the art of polite conversation."

Roger stifled the urge to laugh out loud. This scolding from a woman who'd barely spoken a civil word to their guests and certainly hadn't made them feel welcome. "Indeed, sister dear," he added sarcastically. "Spiteful remarks won't endear you to any gentleman."

Philippa squirmed, probably more on account of their mother's unusual rebuke. "Who says I want to marry a gentleman?"

Roger narrowed his eyes. "Perhaps you don't," he replied.

"But you have expensive tastes, and rich men have their pick of any number of potential brides."

The moment the words were out of his mouth, he realized his mistake. His mother's satisfied nod confirmed it. He was still a relatively rich man, but wouldn't be for long if the famine continued and the murder investigation dragged on. He'd been in a state of uncomfortable arousal since basking in the glow of Beatrice's smile. However, now was the time to marry a woman with a large dowry, not the daughter of the heir to an impoverished barony. "I'm for bed, if you'll excuse me," he said, suspecting Beatrice would haunt his thoughts and he'd get very little sleep this night.

BEA LAY awake for hours struggling to resolve the enigma of Roger Sandiford. The family had wealth, but she deduced from the conversation that something threatened that wealth. Why had a policeman been in the house? She'd seen little evidence of productivity at the mill itself. Yet the workers weren't on strike. She resolved to ask her father's opinion on the matter in the morning.

The possibility of Roger Sandiford's ruin tightened her throat. Despite her determination to treat him coolly, she liked him. He was justifiably proud of what he'd achieved. She knew nothing of his background, though his mother and sister didn't strike her as well born or bred. The fisticuffs episode she'd witnessed spoke of street violence, a circumstance of which she had no experience.

Industrial Lancashire was a far cry from rural Dorset. Perhaps once the Grange was restored, life on the isolated moor would be more settled and peaceful. The prospect did little to bring on the sleep she desperately sought.

She thought she'd only just fallen asleep when Glenda bustled into her bedchamber with a cup of hot chocolate.

"Morning, Miss Beatrice. There's been a murder," her maid exclaimed.

Still half asleep, Bea sipped the beverage while Glenda chattered on. "Wait, what?" she asked, when the word *murder* finally penetrated her tired brain.

"A young lad, beaten to death in the mill a few days ago."

Bea dismissed the notion. Glenda was known to exaggerate things. "Surely not. Who told you this?"

"It's all the servants can talk about. They think the boy's father did it, and I agree. What would you like to wear today?"

The chocolate suddenly tasted like mud. Sandiford must be terribly worried by this unfortunate event. Violence seemed to be all too prevalent in the north. She'd seen for herself how violent the mill's master could be if provoked.

Chapter 8

The Tour

It took Roger a few days to assemble a gang to work on rehabilitating the Grange. He was paying wages to spinners and weavers who had little work in the mill, so he recruited men from among them who had carpentry or gardening experience and women willing to clean.

He therefore spent most of his time in the mill, hoping to minimize contact with Beatrice Parker. He was becoming far too preoccupied with her.

What spare time he had was taken up by Halliwell and the ongoing interviews. He felt very uncomfortable throughout Miles Smethurst's questioning. Miles was either too honest for his own good or he was guilty. He admitted often wishing he could get rid of Malcolm Pickering and that he owned a hammer—but there was nothing untoward in that. Miles was often called upon to tinker with various pieces of machinery that needed attention. Nevertheless, Halliwell insisted Miles produce the hammer which he promptly confiscated because it had what looked like blood on one end. Miles' insistence it was rust carried no weight.

Anxious to get the machines running again, Roger asked

permission to reopen the spinning room. To his surprise, his request was granted.

The same day, Arthur Parker reminded him of their agreement for a tour of the mill and he could hardly refuse. He was dumbfounded and perplexed when Beatrice asked to accompany her father. Mrs. Parker had yet to emerge from her sickbed.

Father and daughter were intelligent and would quickly realize the mill wasn't operating at full tilt. Neither the murder nor the cotton famine was Roger's fault. He had no control over the outcome of the American war, and could only hope Halliwell found the killer quickly. Yet, pride stood in the way of admitting his business might fail if things didn't improve soon. He doubted the Parkers had money, but impressing them might be a solution if it turned out they were wealthy. He operated and lived in mortgaged premises—an unfortunate necessity when he was first starting up the mill. If he couldn't make the payments ...

The day before the tour, he arranged with Billy Wiggins to have the spinning room going full throttle to process what little raw cotton remained on the loading dock.

"Tha's sure?" Wiggins asked. "There'll be nowt left."

Roger realized it was folly, but it was likely he'd soon have to lay off most of his workforce in any case. "I'm sure. Let's show these southerners what a busy Lancashire mill looks like."

"Aw reet," Wiggins replied. "I'll see to it. By the way, I told yon peeler I were glad to see the back o' that bugger Pickering. I gave 'im me 'ammer afore he asked fer it."

Surprised by this revelation, Roger asked, "You've been interviewed?"

"I tracked 'im down. Smethurst told me Halliwell asked fer 'is 'ammer, so I took mine wi' me. Can't be too careful wi' them coppers."

⁓

NERVOUS ABOUT THE tour planned for the following day, and anxious to understand the industry that was the lifeblood of Lancashire, Bea approached her father after dinner. "Papa, have you noticed there doesn't seem to be much going on at the Broadclough mill?" she asked.

His nose remained buried in the newspaper he was reading in their sitting room. "Don't worry your pretty head about it," he muttered.

Annoyed by the unusual patronizing remark, she pressed on. "If I'm to fit into this new world, I need to know what's going on."

He lowered the newspaper and peered at her. "According to reports in the newspapers, there's a shortage of raw cotton. I've been following the story since I learned we were coming to Lancashire."

"I don't understand," she replied.

"There's no cotton being imported from America because of the civil war there."

"Surely that's not the only country that grows cotton?"

"No, Egypt and India supply cotton, but Americans grow the best crop for spinning and weaving. Unfortunately, it's grown in the south, where the fighting is taking place."

"I understand the war is over the issue of slavery."

"Well, I think there are many issues, but the south wants to secede from the Union, principally so it can keep using slaves. The large cotton plantation owners depend on slave labor."

Bea shivered. She'd never thought about how the cotton garments she wore came into being. "But if there's no cotton, how can Sandiford's mill survive?"

"It can't, unless he has machinery that can be adapted to spin the inferior cottons. However, there is a wider problem."

Bea felt heartsick, but at least her father was willing to credit her with enough intelligence to discuss such matters. Most men thought women incapable of understanding world affairs. "Which is?"

"The last few years have seen a boom in the cotton industry. I suspect therein lies Sandiford's success. But the unprecedented growth produced a glut of woven cotton. Prices collapsed worldwide."

"So, even if the mill has cotton, the finished goods are worth a lot less."

"Bright girl," he replied, with an indulgent smile. "India is the biggest importer of printed cottons, but there are apparently warehouses in Bombay full of unsold cloth."

They sat in silence for a few minutes, until her father lowered his paper again and said, "There's something else you should be aware of."

"Glenda was gossiping about a murder, but I didn't think it could be true," she said, alarmed by his deep frown.

"Unfortunately, it is. Don't tell your mother, but a boy's body was found in the spinning room here. The police are investigating."

"That's terrible. I understand many children are injured in the course of their work in the mills. Why do they believe he was murdered?"

"His skull had been caved in, possibly by a hammer."

Shocked to the core by the revelation, Bea now understood the presence of the policeman she'd seen. She worried for Roger Sandiford and what this might mean for his mill. He'd obviously wanted to keep the news from her family. The knowledge there was a murderer at large was unsettling.

With a heavy heart, she looked in on her mother then retired to bed, but she lay awake worrying for Roger Sandiford and wishing she hadn't insisted on joining the tour. It was no wonder his mother was so antagonistic. She must be aware of the threats to her son's empire.

~

DESPITE THE RAMIFICATIONS, Roger's pride soared when he entered the spinning room of his mill the next day, Arthur and Beatrice Parker in tow. The roar and click of the spinning machines were deafening, the cotton dust like a blinding blizzard. Miss Parker wrinkled her nose and covered her mouth with a kerchief, but for Roger, it was like returning to the good days. The noise of a spinning mill operating at full capacity was the sound of prosperity. Music to his ears.

The same contentment lit the faces of the spinners. The resumption of work seemed to have put new energy into the limbs of the *little piecers* crawling beneath the spindles to reattach broken threads.

Miss Parker frowned as she watched the children narrowly escape the machine when it moved back and forth. He anticipated a scolding about employing children to do dangerous work. Who else was small and agile enough to do the job? Thankfully, Malcolm's blood had been scrubbed from the planked floor. Roger hoped she hadn't learned of the murder.

The noise rendered it impossible to explain what was happening, so Roger simply let the visitors watch the spun thread being wound onto the cops.

Miss Parker's keen eyes missed nothing. He'd wager she quickly understood how the spinning mules worked.

When he ushered them out into the yard, she proved eager to pepper him with questions. The heat in the spinning room had reddened her beautiful face. Flecks of cotton dust lay trapped like snowflakes in her burnished tresses. The temptation to take her in his arms and kiss her silly was powerful, but she'd probably slap him.

"Why are the machines called mules?" she asked.

Her question dragged him back to reality. "A local man by the name of Samuel Crompton invented the prototype by combining two earlier inventions. The mule results from the mating of a horse with a donkey, so ..."

"I see," she replied, her blush deepening. "So, can your mules be adapted to spinning other kinds of raw cotton, now there's none coming from America?"

Roger realized he'd fooled nobody with this unwise demonstration, least of all Miss Beatrice Parker. "Unfortunately not," he replied. "The fibers of Indian cotton are too short and break too easily. It would be impossible to provide enough humidity to prevent that from happening."

"And I suppose producing goods made with inferior Indian cotton won't solve the problem of the glut on the market."

Roger chuckled inwardly. This remarkable young woman might turn out to be as astute as his mother. He normally had no time for women who thought themselves the equal of men, but Beatrice Parker's perceptive intelligence only increased his desire for her.

"Is the spinning room where they found the murdered boy's body?" she asked.

"It is," he replied, effecting an air of nonchalance. He should have known the secret would leak out. The killing had been reported in the local newspaper and Arthur was keen to read it every day. "On another matter, I've assembled a crew to work on Belmont Grange. They'll start tomorrow."

Her green eyes widened, but she made no comment about the abrupt change of subject. "That's wonderful. I'd like to go with them to make sure they know what I have in mind for improvements."

Roger's throat tightened. He couldn't allow her to go alone with a gang of workers. "Splendid," he replied. "We'll go in my brougham."

She hesitated. "That's generous of you. We'll take Glenda too."

It was only to be expected the maid would come along as a chaperone. He should be glad. Spending time alone in a vehicle with him would ruin Miss Parker's reputation and stretch his restraint to the limits.

Chapter 9

Beyond Repair

Glenda was not a small woman. Her bulk took up most of one bench in the carriage. Bea couldn't very well sit next to Sandiford, nor could he be expected to squeeze in with Glenda, so Bea sat beside her. The hint of a smile tugging at Sandiford's lips confirmed she looked ridiculous squashed up in a corner of the brougham.

His nose twitched, indicating that he too found the aroma of the maid's *eau de toilette* overwhelming.

Unfortunately, her garrulous maid evidently couldn't resist bringing up the investigation into the murder. "Who do you think did it, Mr. Sandiford?" she asked.

Bea cringed. "I'm sure the police would prefer Mr. Sandiford not discuss the matter."

"And such a violent crime isn't a topic for ladies to discuss," he added.

"Well," Glenda went on undaunted. "The servants reckon Mr. Smethurst did it. And I agree."

Bea couldn't resist a chuckle. "You told me you thought Pickering had killed his own son."

"But that was before the police confiscated Smethurst's hammer."

"They also have Billy Wiggins' hammer," Sandiford told them. "What do you make of that, Miss Glenda?"

Eyes wide, Bea's maid folded her arms across her copious bosom and sulked.

It was tempting to laugh at the absurdity of the situation. As if a respectable man and woman couldn't undertake a short journey without a chatty servant as chaperone. However, she suspected that even in the north, people would frown upon such a circumstance.

In the few days she'd been in Bolton, she'd learned the conservative Wesleyans largely dictated what was socially acceptable.

The more time she spent with Roger Sandiford, the more she liked him. He was an intelligent and successful man of the world, and there were a thousand questions she thirsted to ask him. Conversations among her sewing circle in Dorset consisted almost entirely of cooking tips, cake recipe exchanges, and the latest colors of embroidery silks.

But Glenda would disapprove. Young ladies didn't fraternize with members of the opposite sex.

She closed her eyes and smiled when the notion of vibrant colors brought Odlum's bright yellow pantaloons to mind.

DESPITE THE UNWELCOME presence of the maid, Beatrice Parker's closeness to Roger had resulted in a state of pleasant arousal—until she closed her eyes and smiled. His cock immediately rose to the occasion, a circumstance his long frock coat fortunately hid from Glenda. He'd wager the portly maid knew a thing or two about the male body.

He wondered what thoughts had prompted Miss Parker's smile. Was she dreaming of kissing him? He licked his lips, praying it might be so. If he kissed her, would she allow his hand to wander to a generous breast? He'd wager it would fill his hand nicely.

The maid's loud cough caused Miss Parker's eyes to fly open and brought him back to his senses. Years of struggling to succeed in the competitive world of industry had taught him rigid self-discipline, and he quickly banished carnal thoughts. If only persuading his cock to calm itself were as easy, especially with the object of his desire within reach. "Not far now," he declared, taking out his pocket watch as if he cared about the time.

Five minutes later, they came to a halt in front of the Grange. The workers had already started clearing away some of the overgrown wildflowers and weeds.

"Lord God Almighty," Glenda declared, as she peered out the window.

"You should have seen it before," Miss Parker replied, bestowing a knowing smile on Roger that only hardened his arousal further.

His footman lowered the carriage steps. Roger stepped down quickly and offered his hand to Beatrice before the servant had a chance to assist her. "Let him help the maid," he thought unkindly, as Miss Parker accepted his hand.

Their eyes met when her feet touched the ground. So much for controlling carnal thoughts and his unruly manhood. Certain of an unspoken attraction in her green eyes, he offered his arm. "Allow me to escort you," he said, all his financial troubles pushed aside when she linked her arm in his.

～

Marcus found the encounter with Billy Wiggins somewhat amusing. The fellow sought him out and handed over his hammer without being asked! However, his actions could be a ploy. He was another employee who hated Malcolm Pickering. The lad seemed to have got up everyone's nose. Could Wiggins have struck out at the victim in a moment of blind rage? Try as he might, Marcus couldn't imagine the affable spinners' gaffer resorting to violence.

He made a mental note to track down John Smythe. Several people had mentioned him as a possible suspect because Sandiford had sacked him for smoking. How Smythe's resentment might be connected to the killing had yet to be established.

When they entered the Grange, Bea reluctantly let go of Roger Sandiford's arm. There was a certain rightness about walking arm in arm with him, as if ... but she mustn't let her thoughts wander in that direction. It would be too easy to come to rely on his solid strength, on his charm, on his crooked smile and beguiling dark eyes.

They were from different worlds, and the gap would only widen once her father took up his position as Baron Belmont. Besides which, there was trouble brewing in the cotton industry, and she didn't know enough about the local community to be embroiled in solving problems she didn't fully understand. A shortage of work meant unrest. The Grange might be the safest place to be with a killer on the loose.

When Sandiford excused himself to check on men working on the windows, she approached three women on their knees scrubbing layers of grime on the tiled floor in the foyer. One of them looked pale and haggard. She had a persistent cough that reminded Bea of the tour. They immediately scrambled to their feet and bobbed a curtsey. "Don't leave off on my account," she told them. "I don't envy you the task of cleaning this place."

"Seen worse, miss," the young woman with the cough replied, as they knelt to their task once more.

There was something vaguely familiar about the girl. "I'm Beatrice Parker. Didn't I see you in the mill the other day?" she asked, extending a hand. Women exchanging handshakes was a curious northern custom she felt she should adopt.

"Aye, Bridget Mann," the girl replied, accepting the gesture with surprising strength.

About to continue the conversation, Bea was thrown off guard when Glenda seized her arm and pulled her away. "Don't try to befriend them," the maid cautioned. "You're the baron's daughter and they're working-class skivvies. Besides, one of them could be the murderer."

Hoping the three women hadn't heard the insulting remarks, Bea was irritated by the snobbery of a woman who'd spent her life in service. Glenda's opinion of the killer's identity changed by the moment. Nevertheless, she deemed the busy foyer an unsuitable place to start an argument with Glenda, who evidently considered herself superior to local working women.

She decided to wander through the main rooms of the house, relieved when Glenda marched off, having declared a desire to inspect the kitchens.

In the drawing room, Bea came across Sandiford. He was watching men installing new panes of glass in the large windows. "Splendid," she declared. "This room will benefit from the light."

"Aye, miss," one fellow replied as he removed his cloth cap. "We're grateful to thee and Mr. Sandiford fer givin' us extra work."

Bea's legs trembled. How could she have been so obtuse? It

had never occurred to her someone must be footing the bill for all this work. In Dorset, parishioners had often done odd jobs for the local vicar without expecting payment. More importantly, she had a new appreciation for Sandiford. He cared about his workers. He couldn't give them work in the mill, so he was paying them to assist her family. But pride obliged her to make a ridiculous offer. "I'll speak to my father about defraying your expenses," she told Sandiford, knowing full well her parents had little money.

His smile fled and she realized belatedly that she'd injured his pride. "That won't be necessary," he retorted, his tone as starched as his winged collar.

ROGER OFTEN CURSED his stubborn pride, a sin Miss Parker was also guilty of. He doubted her father had money to spare. Neither did he, yet he gleefully agreed to cover the cost of new curtains for all the rooms when Miss Parker lamented the woeful state of the moth-eaten rags hanging at the windows.

He had to admire the way she went from room to room, cheerfully insisting the house would be a fine place to live once the grime was removed. She examined ancient pieces of furniture and declared they'd prove to be marvelous antiques once they were restored. He'd have consigned the whole decrepit lot to the rag-and-bone men. Philippa would faint dead away if he suggested she live at Belmont Grange.

Beatrice Parker was made of sterner stuff than he'd given her credit for.

An easy camaraderie blossomed between them as they toured the old house. They laughed at the same things. He'd later regret letting his guard down and giving voice to his feelings. "I'm becoming very fond of you, Beatrice," he confessed, taking hold of her hand and raising it to his lips. "More than fond."

He bristled when she snatched her hand away.

"Come now, Mr. Sandiford," she replied haughtily. "A gentleman would never say such things to a lady."

Roger clenched his jaw, seething at the insult. "You find it offensive that I've revealed my feelings?"

"Surely you don't think there can be anything between us. We should return to town. I'll fetch Glenda."

Roger fumed. As far as he was concerned, that was the last blow he'd ever allow Miss Parker to deliver to his pride.

Chapter 10

Regrets

Bea couldn't understand why she felt it necessary to humiliate Roger Sandiford. She liked him. In fact, her feelings were stronger than simply liking. There was an undeniable attraction she'd not felt for a man before. The light brush of his lips on the back of her hand had sent pleasant sensations rippling to her very core. His subtle cologne did strange things to her insides. Yet, she'd rebuffed his advances and made him feel unworthy.

To make matters worse, she'd have to endure the ride back to town with a man she'd angered.

Thankfully, Glenda came to her rescue. "I'll stay," the maid said. "Do a bit to help, then I can ride back in the wagon with the workers."

Bea found it slightly amusing that Glenda suddenly didn't mind traveling with "working class skivvies," but here was her opportunity to avoid Roger Sandiford. "I'll stay with you. Between us we can make sure the work meets our standards."

She could only be grateful Sandiford wasn't within earshot of the pompous statement.

He merely shrugged when she informed him of her decision

to stay. Standing at the weathered front door, she watched his elegant carriage disappear down the rutted track, unable to shake the uneasy feeling she had made a big mistake.

As THE BROUGHAM lurched its way along the moorland path, Roger tried to sort out his feelings. Women were generally flattered when he paid attention to them. His mother told him they were drawn by his dark good looks and brooding countenance, whatever that meant.

He sometimes suspected women were more interested in his wealth than in him.

Obviously, Miss Parker didn't find him or his money attractive. That truth stung more painfully than it should. She evidently considered him beneath her.

His mind wandered. He actually wouldn't object to being beneath her, gripping her hips as she rode him.

This preoccupation with the chit had to stop. There were more important things to worry about than a woman who seemed intent on spinsterhood. Money was going to be a problem. It wasn't likely Philippa would mend her spendthrift ways. He'd foolishly agreed to foot the bill for the ongoing expenses at the Grange. Revenue from the mill was dwindling and would soon dry up altogether. He'd already used up most of his reserves keeping the mules spinning.

Understandably, Pickering's murder had unsettled workers who already had enough to be concerned about. There'd be unrest if he had to lay off his workforce. The solution was to provide them with alternative work, but he no longer had sufficient funds to finance such schemes for long.

Upon his return home, his mother greeted him. "Why the long face?" she asked, as he loosened his neckcloth.

She knew him too well, but he wasn't ready to tell her about Miss Parker's rejection. Instead, he broached the matter of the mortgages on the mill and the house.

"Things are that desperate?" she asked.

"I'm afraid so, Mama," he replied. "We could lose the house. The problem will be compounded when some of our unemployed tenants default on the mortgages I hold on their homes. Others won't be able to pay rents on my properties."

"We'll survive," she replied, supportive as always. "At least we won't go hungry."

Silence followed. They'd both known the gnawing pain of hunger. "No, things aren't that bad. However, most of our workers will have no money for food if we close the mill. I'm resolved to push the topic of forming a relief committee at the next meeting of the mill owners."

"You can try," she replied. "Hampson won't agree. Now, what else is troubling you?"

"Miss Parker won't have me," he sighed, knowing his mother would badger him until he confided the reason for his melancholy. "She finds me offensive."

"Then she's a fool," Lucinda replied. "Who is she to reject you? I hate her for it."

Roger wanted to hate Beatrice Parker, but knew he could not. "I do not wish her spoken of again in this house," he said flatly.

THE RIDE back to town in the crowded wagon was an uncomfortable experience Bea could have done without. Exhausted after scrubbing, sweeping, and cleaning most of the day, she was grateful Glenda's well-padded shoulders provided a cushion when the wagon lurched and rolled. She supposed the unpleasant odor of unwashed bodies was to be expected. The men and women had labored all day. The drizzle didn't help, though the skies cleared miraculously once they left the moor behind.

She was glad of a chance to speak with Bridget Mann, though the girl's cough seemed to be getting worse. "Cotton dust," she explained, thumping her chest.

Bea had spent less than an hour in the spinning room and found it hard to breathe. However, she hadn't given a thought to the consequences for men and women who worked long hours in the mill. "Have you seen a doctor?" she asked.

The disbelief in Bridget's wide eyes said it all, and Bea felt foolish for asking such a question. "I have an elixir. I could bring it to your house."

Bridget looked away, but Bea was determined to do what she could to help. "Tell me the street."

"Red Lane."

"Good. I'll bring it on the morrow."

She dozed for most of the journey as did the workers, though occasional snatches of conversation reached her ears. They speculated about the murder. It seemed they were vehemently opposed to the practice of slavery, but worried about the cotton famine and what it would mean for them. Most were confident Roger Sandiford would look after them.

Their respect for their master only served to convince Bea she'd thrown away any chance of a relationship with a decent man.

Upon arriving back at the Sandiford house, she was pleasantly surprised to find her mother sitting in an armchair in the private sitting room. "You're up," she said with a forced smile. Her mother's skin looked pale and brittle.

"Just for a little while. I suppose I must make the effort."

Having spent hours cleaning the Grange and supervising the workers, Bea knew the true meaning of the word *effort*.

"You look exhausted," her mother remarked.

"Glenda and I worked hard," she replied, desperately trying to temper the resentment bubbling in her throat.

"But there's something else troubling you."

Perhaps her mother was more in touch with reality than she'd thought. "Roger Sandiford made advances," she murmured.

At first, she thought perhaps her mother hadn't heard, but then, "Did you welcome them?"

"I wanted to," she confessed, falling to her knees beside her mother's chair. "But I rejected him."

"There, there," came the reply, as she sobbed into her mother's lap. "The heart usually knows what's best. Things will work out."

Hoping that were true, Bea cherished the calm moments as her mother stroked her hair. Frequent illness had resulted in such closeness happening all too rarely.

Roger's patience was nearing its end. "We've been here in my study for hours," he said to Halliwell. "You've interviewed ten people, including three women, for goodness sake. As if a woman could strike a boy with a hammer."

"You'd be surprised what women are capable of, Mr. Sandiford," the sergeant replied. "But I don't believe Pickering was killed by any of the people we've seen today."

"So, what was the purpose of this wasted time?"

"Good police work takes time and patience, Mr. Sandiford. All today's people worked the same shift as Malcolm Pickering."

"Yes, I realize that."

"They all stated that he was alive when they last saw him at the end of the shift."

Roger rolled his eyes, hoping there was some point to all of this.

"Two or three confirmed the elder Pickering's alibi. They went with him to *The Three Crowns* and stayed there until closing time."

Roger deemed it pathetic that many of his workers preferred to spend hours drinking with cronies instead of going home to their families, although it might be excusable considering the appalling conditions some lived in. But he was glad the father wasn't guilty. "So, what next?"

"We need to question Mrs. Pickering to ascertain if the lad went home or not."

"I should have gone over there before," Roger admitted. "Pay my respects and so on."

"Perhaps we might go together," Halliwell suggested.

Marcus understood Sandiford's impatience. He was getting a bit impatient himself. Tracking down the killer was proving to be more complicated than he at first thought. However, he should pay heed to his own advice. Police work took time and patience.

Smythe was a possibility. Marcus was beginning to suspect the killer was someone from outside Broadclough. The employees he'd interviewed seemed as puzzled as he was. Nobody had pointed the finger. Perhaps a complete stranger had committed the murder. However, the only outsiders he knew of were the new baron and his family but they'd arrived from somewhere in the south of England after the foul deed was done.

Chapter 11

Exploring

The next day, tired of Philippa Sandiford's constant harping on the wonders of London compared to dirty, smelly Lancashire, and feeling the need to exercise muscles aching after the hours spent cleaning, Bea resolved to visit Bridget's home on Red Lane. She explained her mission to Glenda, who thought she'd lost her wits and tried hard to deter her from venturing abroad in this dirty town, especially with a killer roaming the streets.

Bea thought the manner of the boy's death indicated an argument that had gotten out of hand and doubted they'd be accosted even if they met the murderer on the street. She felt she'd won the argument when Glenda agreed to accompany her, first to the International Tea Co. Shop, two streets away from the mill. She was soon glad her maid had come with her. The dozens of men loitering in the streets were polite enough, some even touching their caps when they passed. However, it all felt very foreign and intimidating after the leafy laneways of Milton Abbas, not to mention there was filth and broken pavement underfoot, and the stench was nigh on overwhelming.

The shop's awning proclaimed its owners imported and

distributed provisions from two hundred branches throughout the kingdom. Flies swarmed around two whole sides of bacon propped up on display outside. One window was crammed with slabs of butter, cheese, bacon, and joints of meat. The other window featured an array of various types of tea.

Bea's funds were meager, but she had enough to buy tea, sugar, and rice, with sufficient coin left over to purchase lamp oil. She tucked the provisions into Glenda's basket, alongside the bottle of elixir.

Red Lane wasn't easy to find in the warren of tumbledown tenements. The further they ventured, the narrower the streets. Windows were coated with grime. Many had rags stuffed into broken or cracked panes. They dodged lines of washing strung across from one side of the alley to the other, side-stepped ominous deep puddles, and tried to ignore the incessant wailing of children. A cigarette or pipe dangled from the mouth of every sour-faced man. Every unkempt woman had a wailing baby lashed to her back with a shawl. The street seemed to be the place where laundry was done in large galvanized tubs equipped with washboards. The laundresses worked in a cluster around a lone stand pipe. Idle men leaned on doorways while others played dice.

The two were eyed with suspicion by folk clad entirely in gray clothing beyond repair. Enquiries about the location of the Mann household were answered with grunts and finger-pointing.

The door they finally knocked at was opened by a girl Bea didn't recognize. "I understood Bridget Mann lives here," she tried.

The girl shrugged and disappeared down a flight of stone steps, leaving the door open.

Bea and Glenda entered cautiously, squinting into the dark interior as they navigated the steps.

When their eyes became accustomed to the darkness, they found themselves in a windowless cellar with three people staring at them, Bridget, the girl and an older man.

"We brought you a basket," Bea tried, not certain how to open the conversation.

"We've nowt to put in a basket," Bridget replied hoarsely.

"You misunderstand," Bea said, taking out the packet of tea. "There are things in the basket I thought you might need."

"Don't 'old wi' charity," the man hissed.

"Then you're a stubborn fool," Glenda declared.

A coughing fit seized Bridget, and Bea expected to be ushered out in short order. When she was finally able to breathe, Bridget said, "She's right, Pa. I won't turn me nose up at a good cup o' char."

Sulking, he slumped down in a rocking chair by the cold hearth while Bridget unpacked the basket. "This is me sister, Meg," she wheezed.

Bea extracted the elixir. "Here is the real reason for our visit. I don't like the sound of that cough."

"Nowt to be done 'bout it," Mr. Mann said. "Cotton dust int' lungs."

"Well," Glenda replied. "Won't do the lass any harm to take the medicine."

"Aye, more dangerous out int' street wi' a murderer 'angin' about."

Bea might have known her maid would pursue his statement. "Who do you think is guilty, Mr. Mann?"

"Plain as the nose on tha face. John Smythe kilt the lad."

"The man sacked for smoking?" Bea asked.

"I agree it could be him," Glenda said.

Bea sighed. Her maid was apparently as confused about the murderer's identity as the police.

"Halliwell'll ne'er catch the killer," Mann said. "'E's too slow and steady. Did tha fetch baccy fer rollin' fags?"

"Definitely not," Bea replied, thrown off balance by the abrupt change of subject and bothered by Mann's cryptic remark. "Smoking cigarettes in the house will only worsen Bridget's cough." She refrained from voicing the opinion that the dank place likely wasn't good for the health of the occupants anyway.

His reaction left no doubt about what he thought of his visitors. Snarling, he got up from the chair and stalked out of the house, tripping on the steps as he went.

"Pa'll not give up the fags," Meg said, when the door slammed.

"Then you must take the elixir and walk in the fresh air whenever you can," Bea asserted.

Both girls stared at her. "And where will we find fresh air around 'ere?" Meg asked.

Bea had no answer, so she launched into a monologue about looking forward to moving to Belmont Grange.

"I'm surprised tha wants to leave the Sandifords," Bridget said with a grin.

"Aye," Meg echoed. "I wouldn't mind livin' with a handsome chap like Mr. Sandiford."

Bea's throat tightened. "I'm not living with him, as you put it," she retorted. "The Sandifords have been good enough to put us up while the Grange is being fixed."

"And I'll wager the crafty Mrs. Sandiford is encouragin' tha friendship with 'er son."

"That's utter nonsense. Mr. Sandiford and I are not friends."

Bea found that reality truly depressing.

~

AFTER BEATRICE's rejection of Roger's advances, the Parkers' presence in his home was awkward, but his mother insisted he continue to take his rightful place at the head of the dinner table. The conversation inevitably turned to the murder. Arthur Parker asked if there'd been any progress. Roger gave a brief summary of the interviews he'd witnessed, but refused to express an opinion as to who might be the guilty party.

Beatrice kept her gaze on her plate and remained silent. It irritated Roger that he still craved her, despite her aloofness.

He was taken aback when she suddenly announced she'd ventured into the slums to visit a girl she'd befriended.

"Red Lane?" he exclaimed. "You were lucky to escape in one piece."

"It wasn't that bad," she retorted. "Glenda came with me."

"I say, Bea," her father said, his voice full of disapproval. "Why would you take such a risk?"

"Bridget Mann has a terrible cough, thanks to the cotton dust she inhales working in your mill, Mr. Sandiford. I took her some medicine."

Thunder darkened Lucinda's face. "Miss Parker," she began.

"It's all right, Mother," Roger said. "Miss Parker obviously isn't aware that I have suggested many times that ventilation be installed to clear the air. At my own expense, I might add."

"And?" Beatrice retorted.

"The workers won't have it. The carders at Sutler's Mill complained of hunger as a result of the improved ventilation, arguing that they'd been long used to swallowing fluff and that their wages ought to be raised if they were to work in such places."

Beatrice pursed her lips and thrust out her breasts, only adding to Roger's torment.

"That is no excuse not to improve working conditions," she declared.

"You should keep your nose out of affairs that don't concern you, Miss Parker," Lucinda said. "I am proud of what my son has accomplished with Broadclough."

"If you'll excuse me," Beatrice said, as she rose and flounced out of the dining room.

"Good riddance, Miss La-Dee-Da," Philippa said, with her nose in the air.

Roger heard the sound of another nail being hammered into the coffin of his hopes to woo Beatrice Parker.

SICK AT HEART and suspecting she'd get no sleep, Bea decided to write a letter to her one friend in Dorset. She and Edith Rexton were the only girls of their age in Milton Abbas and had consequently been friends since childhood. Unlike Beatrice, Edith had been quite content to marry a sheep farmer, and hadn't understood the excitement of a new beginning in Lancashire.

It was galling to write about the difficulty of adapting to life in the north. She could imagine Edith's *told you so* reaction.

She had to let somebody know how lonely she was, how isolated she felt, but was it true that she longed to return to Dorset? She did miss long walks across the downs, but walking around Bolton was more—she searched for the right word, finally settling on *exciting*.

She included a lengthy description of Belmont Grange and the work that had to be put into its restoration, briefly mentioning how grateful she was to the Sandifords.

She tried to describe the social divide, the antagonism between workers and masters. Lucinda believed some men were meant to be masters while others would always try to pull them down. It was doubtful Edith would accept that as the way of the world.

In her letter, she complained about the damp northern weather and wrote at length about the appalling working conditions in the cotton mills, but she made no mention of her burgeoning feelings for Roger Sandiford and the mess she'd made of her relationship with him. That ship had sailed.

Chapter 12

Relief

As the mill owners gathered once more at *The Pack Horse*, the tension in the air was palpable. Roger suspected many of his fellow industrialists were facing the same worsening situation with regards to the cotton famine. He assumed the discussion would center around the looming catastrophe of mass layoffs. Instead, he was bombarded with questions about the progress of the murder investigation.

"Nothing much to report," he replied. "The sergeant has interviewed several people, not all of them suspects. As far as I know, he hasn't yet tracked down the culprit."

"But tha must have some idea of who it is," Hampson claimed. "We all know who the bad apples are in our workforce."

"True," Roger conceded. "But I can't think of a single employee of mine who'd stove in a boy's head with a hammer."

"Art insinuating one of our workers did it?" Sutler retorted.

Roger rolled his eyes. "Look, we have more important matters to discuss. What are we going to do about the famine?"

"Nowt fer it but to close the mills," Hampson declared.

"Aye," a few mumbled.

Roger decided he wasn't going to sit by and let his workers starve. "If we do that, we must provide relief for our employees."

"Nay, lad," Hampson replied, in a patronizing tone of voice. "It's every man fer hisself."

Roger rarely challenged Hampson who could be a vindictive sod, but he stuck to his guns. "Our workers have stood by us time and again. They refused to strike when unionists threatened them. Lancashire cotton spinners have sent an official letter to Abraham Lincoln in support of the fight against slavery in America. They've helped all of us become rich. Now, we plan to abandon them? There'll be hell to pay and more than one murder to solve."

"They've made threats?" Hampson growled.

Exasperated, Roger shook his head. "The American war will end one day. Lancashire folk have long memories. Chances are they'll work willingly for masters they respect."

"Well," Hampson groused. "I suppose it'll do no 'arm to write to the Manchester Central Relief Committee. Mebbe they can 'elp. In the meantime, I'm shuttin' down."

Roger suspected the people in Manchester had their hands full assisting unemployed men and women in that city. But he'd said his piece. He could only try to protect his own workers. Lucinda had known hunger. She'd help him set up some sort of kitchen with simple food. It was the least he could do with his meager resources.

Intending to purchase another of Mr. Thornley's pies, he left the meeting and set off to Newport Street. Intent on watching where he stepped, he thought for a moment he espied a man wearing yellow trousers heading for the hotel. It couldn't be the foppish law clerk. He'd gone back to London, and this fellow was deep in conversation with another man. Perhaps yellow was the fashionable thing these days, though Roger would sooner be caught dead than even consider such an ostentatious color.

THE MORNING after her foray into the slums, Bea awoke later than usual. It was the second day in a row she'd slept in. Every part of her body still ached from cleaning the Grange. Shrugging on a wrapper, she found her parents in the sitting room. Her father was hidden behind his newspaper. She wondered how he'd manage out on the moor. It was doubtful the paper would be delivered to the Grange.

Her mother was spooning the last of a boiled egg from an eggcup.

"Looks good," she said. "I'll get Glenda to make me one."

"She left already," her mother announced. "Gone out to the Grange with the crew."

Her father lowered his newspaper. "It's good of Sandiford to foot the bill for the clean-up. I suspect he can ill afford it."

Guilt surged in Bea's throat. She'd more or less cajoled him into paying for new curtains.

"Our daughter rejected his advances the day before yesterday," her mother revealed.

Bea seethed. "I told you that in confidence, Mama."

Her father peered at her over the top of his spectacles. "I suppose you know your own mind, child, but Sandiford's a good man. I'm impressed with his achievements as a self-made man. He pays better wages than most of the other mill owners. You could do worse, although your outburst last evening did little to enamor you to him. He told me earlier this morning that he and his mother are planning to set up a soup kitchen for those he can no longer employ. He's got men refurbishing the idle machinery who otherwise would be out of work."

Bea couldn't change the past, no matter how much she regretted her tendency to always put a foot wrong. She shook off her lethargy. "Surely there's something we can do," she said.

"The women can learn to do fine needlework, like invisible mending," her mother suggested.

"Then they could perhaps find work as seamstresses," Bea replied enthusiastically. "I could teach them."

"And we can give classes in reading and writing," her father said.

"And simple mathematics," Bea agreed, her spirits lifting. If she helped with good works, Roger Sandiford might see she wasn't the snobbish socialite he deemed her to be.

FOR A WEEK, Roger made a point of dropping into the soup kitchen at midday. He noted that the number of workers taking advantage of the free food increased daily. His mother insisted on being present every day to ladle out the soup. She'd never found it easy to socialize with people, so he was proud of her efforts to keep the workers' spirits up. The one topic of conversation was, of course, the murder. The consensus seemed to be that the killer would never be caught. Roger found that prospect disturbing.

Despite the drain on his resources, he was glad they'd set up the kitchen in a storage shed that was no longer needed. The unemployed women who made the soup told him they felt useful again. It was clear the people who came appreciated his efforts, especially those with large families of young children. They were polite and respectful. It might have been a very different story if he'd done nothing. There'd been talk of machine breaking at other mills.

The classes offered by the Parkers had also gone a long way

to relieving tension. Attendance entitled the workers to Poor Law payments. Beatrice was teaching dozens of women the skill of invisible mending. So many had wanted to be included in the literacy and mathematics classes, she and her father had been obliged to limit enrollment to the older boys. Most of them were piecers and little piecers, who might have a better chance of obtaining other employment if they could read and write and do simple sums. It was encouraging to see such a thirst for knowledge and the workers' realization that education meant advancement. Winning a scholarship to Bolton Grammar School for Boys had changed his life.

Roger's home had become a hive of activity. Halliwell informed him he was beginning to think outsiders had killed Malcolm. He no longer needed the study for interviews. It became the location of the mathematics classes. Only Philippa petulantly objected to *commoners* using the drawing room and his study for lessons. Roger had to smile. His sister apparently considered herself a member of the nobility.

Roger stupidly looked forward to spending time in his study in the evening so he could inhale lingering traces of Beatrice Parker's lavender perfume.

Her obvious enjoyment of the classes was commendable. Perhaps she wasn't the stuck-up socialite he'd thought. It was inevitable they bump into each other from time to time. On one occasion, she stammered out an apology for what she called her atrocious manners and lack of gratitude. Each time they met after that, she blushed furiously and couldn't meet his gaze. She took her meals upstairs on a tray, ostensibly to keep her mother company. He began to wonder if she did have feelings for him. Despite his best efforts, his desire for her refused to abate.

Chapter 13

Fire

Bea did her best to avoid Sandiford's mother, who seemed determined to scowl at her each time their paths crossed. She suspected Roger had told her about the incident at the Grange, but didn't know how to explain her foolish reaction to the mother of the man she'd rebuffed. She couldn't explain it to herself. It was uncomfortable living in the house ruled by a woman who clearly held her in low esteem. So much for Meg's assertion Lucinda Sandiford was intent on playing Cupid. The thought should have been amusing but Bea wasn't amused.

On the other hand, Roger's mother seemed to go out of her way to be friendly to Bea's parents, always asking her father about Mrs. Parker's health, and even visiting the sickroom on occasion. She complimented Arthur on the success of his literacy classes. Bea was afforded no such accolades for her sewing and mathematics classes, of which she was justifiably proud.

Annoyed with herself for craving even a word of praise from Sandiford himself, she was surprised when he dropped into the mathematics class unannounced. She and her pupils were in his study, so she could hardly object.

She was unnerved when he folded his arms, braced his long legs, and watched from the rear for a while. He really was a sinfully attractive man. That naughty thought sent icy heat flooding through her veins. She breathed more easily when he turned his attention to the shelves of leather-bound tomes that lined one wall.

She had become fond of his study. This was evidently where he smoked cigars in the evening. The pungent aroma lingered. She pictured him relaxing in one of the red leather armchairs in front of the hearth, perhaps reading a book, perhaps thinking of her—good thoughts, she hoped.

He made decisions in this room, and she didn't envy him the difficult choices he faced now.

The lesson over, she dismissed her students, holding her breath when Sandiford sauntered over to his desk where she was gathering her teaching materials.

"You're a gifted teacher, Miss Parker," he said.

"Thank you," she replied, her heart rejoicing. "I find it helps if I use visual aids they're familiar with."

"Like the cotton cops," he said, holding up one of the spindles wound with thread.

"Yes, I hope you don't mind my borrowing them from the mill. Mr. Smethurst got them for me. He said it would be all right."

"Capital idea," he replied. "Your efforts are helping more than you know. Carry on."

She watched him leave, perplexed by the rapid beating of her heart. Why was she incapable of speaking with Roger Sandiford without craving his kiss?

LEAVING THE STUDY, Roger clenched his jaw. Beatrice Parker and Miles Smethurst? Surely not. His overseer might still be a murder suspect, yet she'd felt comfortable asking him for help. Perhaps the problem wasn't that she considered herself superior, but rather inferior to the likes of a mill owner.

Annoyed to admit feelings of jealousy, he quickly dismissed the preposterous idea, but resolved to keep an eye on Miles Smethurst. He was the only employee still being paid full wages, though he had precious little to do these days. However, he was good at his job. Docking his wages might result in him looking for work elsewhere. When the American war finally ended, Roger didn't want to find himself getting the mill up and running again without an overseer—if the building hadn't been repossessed by the mortgage holder.

At least local troublemakers had stayed away from his factory, thanks he was sure to the relief measures he'd put in place. Or perhaps they were afraid of bumping up against a killer. Rumor had it John Smythe was one of the ringleaders of the unrest. Smythe probably harbored a grudge against Roger for sacking him after the smoking incident. He hoped the fellow wouldn't find support among the workers if he took a notion to suggest an attack against Broadclough. He idly wondered if Smythe had an alibi for the night of the murder, but Halliwell had likely pursued that avenue of inquiry. Nevertheless, it might be as well to double the night watch at the earliest opportunity.

～

BEA HADN'T YET FALLEN asleep, though it must be well past midnight. Earlier in the day, Glenda had reported that Belmont Grange was more or less habitable. Bea welcomed the prospect of moving to a home of her own, but leaving the Sandiford household meant not seeing Roger every day. It also had ramifications for the lessons she conducted. It would be risky to travel into town in the dilapidated carriage they'd found in the derelict stables, and they had no horse in any case.

Strident male voices suddenly broke the silence. Loud footsteps. People running, shouting. She tumbled out of bed when someone rapped on her bedroom door. The cries were louder now. FIRE! FIRE!

"Miss Parker, the mill's on fire. We must get your mother out of the house now."

Hastily shrugging on her wrapper, she cracked open the door. "Roger!" she gasped, her eyes drawn to the smattering of dark curls visible at the open neck of his shirt. It was the first time she'd seen him in shirtsleeves and without a neckcloth. Her mouth fell open as desire rippled through her.

He stared hungrily at her disheveled appearance, longing darkening his narrowed eyes. "Beatrice," he rasped.

The spell was broken when the door to her parents' adjacent room opened. "What's going on?" her father demanded.

Resolute now, Roger strode past him. "We must get Mrs. Parker to safety in case the fire spreads to the house."

"You should be fighting the fire," Bea told him, as she watched him scoop up her mother, counterpane and all, from her sickbed. "We'll take care of ourselves."

Clearly intent on his mission, he ignored her. She and her father followed him downstairs, out of the house and into the mill yard. The housemaids huddled together, the flames from the fire highlighting the fear on their faces. Dressed in her usual black bombazine, Lucinda Sandiford stood apart, stony-faced as ever, a blanket wrapped around her shoulders.

An army of men had formed a line, passing buckets of water.

Roger set Bea's mother on her feet. "I have to go," he shouted over the din.

Bea nodded as she and her father propped up her mother. "We'll see to her."

He ran off to join the fight.

Smoke billowed, making it difficult to breathe. As Bea peered into the gray clouds, it appeared to her that the fire was confined to the storage shed housing the soup kitchen.

Chapter 14

Losses

"The shed's a write-off," Smethurst told Roger the morning after the fire. "We're fortunate the flames didn't get to the mill or the house."

"I don't believe the intention was to destroy the mill," Roger replied, his throat parched by the lingering acrid stink of smoke. "They wanted to send a message to the workers who've come to rely on the soup kitchen."

Smethurst nodded thoughtfully. "Will you start it up somewhere else?"

"Of course," he insisted. "The workers won't see their children go hungry. They'll still come. This is the work of a radical. The way to make sure our workers don't join him is to carry on providing what relief we can."

"Beggin' yer pardon, Mr. Sandiford, but it will all be for naught if the mill's repossessed."

Roger should have been annoyed by his overseer's comment, but the man had been loyal and deserved to know where they stood. "When I made the last mortgage payment, I spoke to the manager at the Westminster Bank. It seems we have a bit of breathing space. The mortgage holder died recently and his heir

95

has yet to be told of his inheritance. Some problem tracking him down."

"So, let's 'ope the Americans come to their senses soon."

"Or God grants us an unexpected windfall. I might have persuaded Joshua Brownlow to release some of the raw cotton he's had in storage in his warehouse. His son's courting my sister."

"I'd sooner depend on the Americans than that greedy bugger. Hoardin' to drive up the value."

"He is demanding a steep price," Roger confessed. "He wants two shillings a pound for cotton he bought for eightpence a pound. Charging three times as much is to be expected from a merchant, I suppose."

They shared unflattering opinions of Joshua Brownlow, even suggesting he was a man capable of murder, but Roger was no closer to knowing if Smethurst was pursuing Miss Parker.

"I suspect John Smythe o' startin' the fire," Miles remarked.

"That will be hard to prove," Roger replied. "The police are having enough trouble tracking down a murderer."

"Aye," Miles agreed. "And they still 'ave me 'ammer. Could Smythe also be the killer?"

Roger found that possibility worrisome.

BEFORE THE FIRE, Bea thought her mother's health was improving. The unfortunate incident took a toll, and Bea could no longer deny Abigail Parker was fading away. It was apparent she'd lost the will to live. Glenda's mournful face confirmed her suspicions. The physician summoned by Lucinda Sandiford shook his head and confessed he wasn't hopeful of a recovery.

In the course of a few days, the cough got worse. Every breath became a wheeze. Waking moments were few and far between. "It's the laudanum," Bea's father insisted, but Bea accepted the real reason. Her mother was slipping away. Her father just didn't want to admit the trek north had irreparably damaged his wife's already fragile health.

The move to Belmont Grange was postponed.

Desperate to escape the pall of impending death hanging over her mother, Bea continued to teach the sewing and mathematics classes. When it became common knowledge that Abigail would never leave her bed, one of the women volunteered to help tend her. "Nursed me own mum at the end," Charity told her.

Worn out and heartsick keeping vigil every night, Bea accepted. She eventually overcame Glenda's strident objections. Convincing her father to leave his wife's bedside was more difficult, but he finally agreed to get some sleep.

Ultimately, the wheezing stopped abruptly in the early afternoon exactly a fortnight to the day after the fire.

Bea grasped her mother's cold hand, raised it to her cheek and wept. Abigail Parker would never stroke her daughter's hair again.

ANOTHER DEATH, this one closer to home, affected everyone in the Sandiford household.

Philippa sulked because the mourning interfered with the planned announcement of her engagement to Josiah Brownlow, son of the merchant hoarding raw cotton.

Lucinda saw it as an ill omen that presaged disaster. She gave up helping with the reestablished soup kitchen, and spent most of the day in her sitting room.

Arthur Parker took his wife's death hard, repeatedly

blaming himself for bringing her north when he knew her health was frail.

Miss Parker seemed determined to put on a brave face, but red-rimmed eyes told of prolonged weeping.

Many of the factory's workers showed up at the door to offer condolences. It was a testament to the affection they felt for Arthur Parker and his daughter. They appreciated the pair's efforts to provide relief at a difficult time.

As for Roger, he longed to take Beatrice into his arms and kiss away the hurt. Having scraped together £25 to make the mortgage payment, and more or less guaranteed of a delay in proceedings if he defaulted next month, he offered to foot the bill for the funeral. The undertaker owed him a few favors.

Standing behind the family in the small cemetery on the windswept moor, he watched Beatrice shiver and sway as her mother's coffin was lowered into the ground. He almost wished she would swoon so he could rush forward and catch her, but acknowledged sadly that she was made of sterner stuff.

He bristled when a young man he didn't recognize stepped forward, put an arm around Beatrice's waist and supported her elbow. He clenched his jaw when she leaned into the stranger, unable to shake the feeling he'd seen the chap before somewhere.

BEA HAD ONLY RECONNECTED with Peter Leigh once since they were children, but she was grateful, if somewhat surprised, her cousin had traveled from London to attend his aunt's funeral. He was rather too citified, too sure of himself for her liking, but he'd made the effort. She hoped he'd come out of duty and not to pursue his astonishing and unlooked-for offer of marriage. Of all the mourners gathered on this cold, damp afternoon, he and Glenda were perhaps the only ones who understood how wrong this all was. Abigail Parker should be laid to rest in the small parish graveyard in her native Dorset, not in a derelict moorland cemetery in Lancashire.

Most of the blackened, indecipherable headstones had toppled over. The only sign anyone had ventured into the small plot was the heap of dirt atop the recently departed Baron Belmont's grave. A simple wooden cross with his name carved into it was the sole indication of who lay buried there. *Algernon Fothergill, Fifth Baron Belmont.*

In the few days since her mistress' death, Glenda had shared poignant memories of first meeting Abigail Parker. Beatrice felt ashamed that she'd never realized the depth of the maid's love.

His wife's death had transformed Bea's father into an automaton. Frowning, he stared into the grave as if he couldn't believe what was happening. He'd barely spoken a word since the fateful day, and had even lost interest in smoking his pipe and reading his newspaper. Bea was grateful to Roger Sandiford, who'd taken upon himself the onus of arranging the funeral. The headstone he'd commissioned lay beside the grave, ready to be set atop it once the earth was shoveled in. *Baroness Abigail Parker* struck her as ludicrous in the circumstances, but Sandiford had meant well.

She sensed Roger's presence behind her, felt it like the pull of a magnet. His mother and sister had also come, though Philippa pouted throughout the uphill trek from the Sandiford brougham.

Bea was about to turn and acknowledge Roger, but Peter stepped forward and kept her upright. Expressing her gratitude would have to wait.

❧

LUCINDA INSISTED the mourners adjourn to her home for tea and sandwiches. She watched over the maids serving the refreshments like a hawk. Roger deemed it unfortunate she didn't speak to Philippa about her rude behavior. His sister's pout and her fiancé's sour face made it clear they didn't want to be there. Josiah Brownlow hadn't even attended the interment. Roger couldn't fathom what Philippa saw in the pimple-faced chap, other than his family's wealth.

He was rather more perturbed by the presence of the man who'd been very familiar with Beatrice at the cemetery and who'd latched on to her like a barnacle. He approached the pair and offered his hand. "Roger Sandiford," he said.

"Peter Leigh," came the response that accompanied a limp handshake. "Miss Parker's cousin."

"Peter came all the way from London," Beatrice explained hesitantly.

"Good of him," Roger replied, pleased that she seemed ill at ease. He wondered why a cousin she obviously barely knew had come all the way to Lancashire to attend a family funeral. He'd evidently felt entitled to put his arm around her at the graveside.

"I hear you've a murderer loose in your mill, Sandiford," Leigh said.

Roger might not belong to the upper class, but he knew enough not to broach such a subject in front of a lady. Nor was it a suitable topic for a first conversation with a stranger. "The police have the matter in hand," he replied.

"Really?" Leigh exclaimed. "I heard Sergeant Plod is floundering."

Beatrice gasped.

Tempted to punch the southerner, Roger gritted his teeth as her cousin wandered off.

"Peter's lodging at *The Pack Horse*," Beatrice explained nervously.

Roger knew the hotel well. Leigh must be fairly wealthy to be staying at the most expensive place in town, but his suspicions were instantly forgotten when she laid her gloved hand atop his arm. "Please accept my thanks for arranging everything, Mr. Sandiford."

He couldn't help himself. He took her into his arms, inhaled her perfume and murmured, "You're welcome."

He expected a hasty retreat and a stern rebuke. Instead, she melted into him, and his heart and body rejoiced.

Chapter 15

Moving Day

Two days after the funeral, Bea, her father, and Glenda moved to Belmont Grange. They possessed no furniture and had never fully unpacked, so there was only luggage and boxes of books to transfer. Roger Sandiford arranged for a wagon to transport trunks, valises, and new bedding he'd purchased. Glenda traveled in the wagon which had left earlier. Roger provided his brougham for Bea and her father. Peter arrived from his hotel and accompanied them, though Glenda muttered she would have appreciated his assistance with the luggage.

Bea felt bad that she still hadn't apologized to Roger for her unseemly behavior at the funeral, and it appeared she wouldn't get a chance on the journey. In truth, she didn't regret depending on his solid strength. It felt good to be held in this man's arms.

Arthur Parker had shrunk to a shadow of his former self. All her life, Bea had known him as the outgoing, erudite member of the family. Grief and loss had stolen his love of conversation. He took the seat next to Sandiford, and Bea sat beside Peter. The heat of embarrassment rose in her face when her chatterbox cousin slithered his arm around her shoulder.

If she harbored any doubts that Roger Sandiford had feelings for her, they flew away like chaff on the wind when he fisted his hands, clenched his jaw, and glared at her cousin. Peter chattered on, seemingly unaware he was acting inappropriately in front of her father. She wondered again why he'd come north for the funeral of an aunt he didn't know and whose death hadn't dampened his high spirits.

"I'm looking forward to seeing this estate of yours, Uncle," he told Bea's father, who made no reply.

Sandiford frowned. Was he perhaps also curious about her cousin's motives? She'd written to inform her aunt of her sister's death, but hadn't contemplated she would send her son north.

"Don't get your hopes up," she replied. "Mr. Sandiford's workers have made a lot of improvements, but ..."

"Good of you, Sandiford," Peter drawled, looking out of the window. "What a barren landscape," he declared, with more than a hint of condescension.

On her first visit to the moor, Bea had thought the same thing. Suddenly, she felt perversely protective of the rocky plateau she would henceforth call home. "If you look carefully, you'll see it's not as barren as you think," she replied, deliberately staring into Roger's eyes. "Things are not always as they seem."

ROGER TOOK heart from Beatrice's assertion. She was growing fond of the wild moors he'd loved since he was a child. Could it be she was also growing fond of him? What was the message in those intriguing green eyes?

She'd permitted him to embrace her at the wake after the funeral, but perhaps that was simply a way of assuaging her grief. Did she regret allowing him to hold her?

For him, the embrace was a magical experience that had predictably aroused his body. But his soul had rejoiced too. This woman was made for him, but did she feel the same?

He admired how elegant she looked in black. Mourning attire didn't compliment most redheads. Beatrice Parker was the exception.

He narrowed his eyes at the man sitting opposite. If Peter Leigh didn't soon get his paws off the woman he loved ...

"Here we are," Beatrice said, as the carriage jolted to a halt.

"Good grief, Cuz," Peter declared, finally removing his arm. "You can't live in this ruin."

"Of course we can," she replied, in a haughty tone that was music to Roger's ears. She had no love in her heart for this cousin.

He tamped down his irritation when Peter lunged for the door, leaped from the carriage and insisted on assisting Beatrice to alight. He then offered his arm and escorted her into the house, leaving Roger fuming as he helped Arthur Parker from the brougham.

BEATRICE WAS DISAPPOINTED it wasn't Roger Sandiford escorting her into her new home. Peter was family, but she felt no kinship with him. By rights, Roger should be escorting her and her father into the house. She'd envisaged the scene many times. He'd seen the house at its very worst, whereas Peter ...

"Great Caesar's ghost," her cousin declared upon entering the foyer. "Ghastly."

Her patience at an end, she unhooked her arm from his. "This is my home, Peter. The house may have its shortcomings, but it has character that comes along with an interesting history."

She didn't yet know what that history might turn out to be, but her cousin wasn't aware of that.

"Are you trying to make a stuffed bird laugh, Cuz?" Peter replied with a grin. "You're barking at a knot."

Bea had no idea what he meant, but she'd had enough of Peter's clever London slang. She turned back to meet her father, relieved to see he was being escorted through the entryway by Mr. Sandiford.

Glenda rushed into the foyer. Ignoring Peter, she immediately took over from Roger. "I've a nice cozy bed all ready for you to have a lie down, sir," she told Bea's father. "Mr. Sandiford's crew have worked wonders with this place."

It might have been Bea's imagination, but she could have sworn the maid winked at Sandiford before turning to Peter.

"Mr. Leigh," Glenda cajoled. "Can you help me get your uncle up the stairs?"

ROGER SMILED. He had an unlikely ally in his pursuit of Miss Parker! "Do you think they can manage?" he asked, as the trio made its way one slow step at a time.

"Glenda could have managed by herself," Beatrice replied. "She evidently doesn't think it inappropriate you and I are left alone."

At first he wasn't sure if she was being serious, but her wide grin soon set him straight.

"Let's explore," she declared.

Roger was more interested in exploring Beatrice Parker's

tempting body, but that wasn't going to happen—yet. "Where do you want to start?" he asked.

"I'd like to see the new curtains in the sitting room," she replied.

"Lead on," he indicated with an exaggerated bow.

He stood behind her as she spread her arms wide in front of the windows.

"What a difference good quality draperies make!" she exclaimed.

Roger's cock urged him to put his arms around her, nuzzle her neck, and cup her lovely breasts, but she changed her stance and turned to face him. "Mr. Sandiford, I can't thank you enough for all the money and effort you've put into renovating this house," she told him.

"I'd do anything to make you happy, Beatrice," he replied, seemingly incapable of holding on to his resentment. "I wish you would call me Roger."

Bea was on dangerous ground. She loved spending time with Roger Sandiford and sharing laughter with him, but he was sending out unmistakably sensuous signals. He wanted her. She'd struggled to deny that she also had feelings for him, but the desire to let him hold her again was overwhelming. "Roger," she began.

Perhaps it was something in her voice that alerted him to her feelings. He strode forward and took her into his embrace. "May I kiss you?" he asked.

He might not be a gentleman in the traditional sense of the word, but he'd behaved in a most gentlemanly manner ever since they'd first met. "Yes," she whispered in reply.

"What ho?" Peter shouted from the foyer. "Where are you, Cuz?"

Deflated, she looked into Roger's laughing eyes and saw the promise of future kisses.

Chapter 16

Whirlwind Of Events

S ubsequent events conspired to keep Roger occupied for several days. The soup kitchen became busier. His mother finally relented and took over supervision of the preparation and distribution of bread and soup. Beatrice continued the classes in sewing and mathematics. She also assumed her father's role and helped those wishing to learn to read and write. Roger saw her briefly when their paths happened to cross. His brougham whisked her back to Belmont Grange at dusk each day.

Roger cursed Peter Leigh. But for his untimely intervention at the Grange, he'd have kissed Beatrice and made sure she understood he loved her. As it was, the pesky cousin occasionally came into town with Beatrice. At first, he showed great interest in the running of the mill, peppering Roger with all kinds of questions. He lost interest when it became obvious the mill was mostly idle.

Shortly after that, Halliwell questioned Roger about his movements the night of the murder. He claimed to have it on good authority that Roger had worked late in the mill. He refused to name his source but quickly accepted Lucinda's confirmation that Roger had worked in his study in the house well into the night.

Roger couldn't rid himself of the nagging suspicion Leigh was the *reliable source*, though he'd purportedly arrived in Bolton a good while after the murder. Beatrice's cousin was up to something. If he'd come north in the hopes of profiting from his uncle's elevation to the nobility, he was sadly mistaken. The Parkers were not wealthy and neither was the Belmont barony. That unfortunate truth brought a measure of comfort, but why would he want to throw suspicion onto Roger?

The Londoner seemed to have made himself at home at Belmont Grange. Roger couldn't bear the thought of the toff and Beatrice spending evenings together.

He became involved in the hunt for John Smythe when the latter and his gang were seen setting fire to the pump-house at Hampson's mill. Roger personally thought Smythe had cut his own throat by tangling with Hampson, whose influence brought the entire Lancashire constabulary into the manhunt.

Within a week, the firebrand and his gang were rounded up in Daubhill and sent to the Manchester Assizes for trial, after Halliwell had satisfied himself he wasn't the killer. Smythe had apparently been setting another fire on the night in question. He probably didn't realize how lucky he was that Hampson's vigilantes hadn't found him first.

In the midst of all this drama, Philippa confided to Lucinda that she was with child. A marriage was hastily arranged and guests invited to a celebratory ball to be held at Sandiford Manor. Roger dreaded the extra expense, though Joshua Brownlow released a quantity of raw cotton from his warehouse. "The least I can do," Joshua told Lucinda, who promptly chastised him for his son's transgression.

Roger hoped he'd have a chance to confess his love when Beatrice came to the ball.

THE MORE MARCUS HALLIWELL thought about it, the odder it seemed that Mr. Peter Leigh had felt it necessary to throw suspicion for the murder on Roger Sandiford. The chap hadn't even been in Bolton when Pickering was killed, so how could he be aware of Sandiford's movements on the night in question?

Marcus had never for a moment suspected the mill's owner, and he'd felt mighty uncomfortable questioning him, but what choice did he have? He had to follow every lead. The superintendent had warned him about offending Sandiford. He hoped his superiors never got wind of it.

It might be worth looking into Leigh, though there was no reason to investigate a man who'd mentioned several times that he'd been in London at the time of the murder.

IN BEATRICE'S OPINION, the only benefit to her cousin's continued presence at Belmont Grange was that his non-stop chatter gradually coaxed her father out of his stupor.

She found herself unexpectedly comfortable in the ramshackle house. She even got used to the cats Roger had procured. When she wasn't offering theories on the identity of the murderer, Glenda, too, bustled about as if she were a servant in some grand mansion. There were still a lot of shortcomings, and the place was drafty, but it had good bones. Sitting by the hearty coal fire, she watched smoke curl into the newly-swept chimney, and filled her head with the prospect of one day restoring the Grange to its former glory. Perhaps when the cotton famine was over and Roger's fortunes reestablished ...

It was a fanciful notion. Sandiford might be attracted to her now, but her late mother had warned that men's affections didn't last once they had taken what they wanted. She couldn't picture Roger behaving in such a devious manner, but it would be well to be wary. She had no experience of men, and Lancashire was very different from Dorset. She assumed self-made men like Roger had to be ruthless in their dealings with others.

The invitation to Philippa Sandiford's wedding celebration came as a surprise. She and Brownlow's son had only been engaged for a short time. They struck Bea as a mismatched pair. Roger's sister was outgoing, frivolous, and clearly ambitious. Josiah Brownlow was gangly, awkward, and plain as dishwater. He had one of those prominent Adam's apples that attracted the eye and sickened the stomach when it bobbed up and down. Bea suspected it was the father's fortune that drew Philippa. A knot tightened in her belly when she considered Roger might be pushing his sister to marry Josiah in order to alleviate the Sandiford family's current financial woes. It was unlikely the head-strong Philippa Sandiford could be forced to do anything, but the possibility was perhaps another reason to be wary of Roger's advances. Bea was completely out of her depth in this game of romance. The last few weeks had consisted of a whirlwind of exhausting events. She'd never attended a ball and longed to go to the wedding celebration, but it might be as well to decline the invitation. After all, she and her father were in mourning, and a killer was still free.

WHEN THE PARKERS declined the invitation to Philippa's celebration, Roger was keenly disappointed but he understood. They were still in mourning. It didn't lessen his craving. Watching Philippa and Josiah exchange vows, he wished with all his heart that he and Beatrice were the couple standing before the minister.

As the ball got underway, he was exchanging small talk with the newlyweds when his sister declared, "Well, if it isn't Miss Holier-Than-Thou herself."

Roger's body and heart reacted predictably when he turned to see Beatrice Parker. Even dressed in a simple black gown, she was the most beautiful woman in the room. Her odious cousin was her escort, but Roger knew she didn't care much for Peter, so he dismissed a pang of jealous annoyance and rushed to greet them. "Welcome," he gushed, bestowing a courtly kiss on Beatrice's knuckles and forcing himself to shake Leigh's hand. "I understood you weren't coming."

"Papa won't be joining us," she replied. "But Peter insisted we come."

Thank you, Peter.

"What a magnificent room," she exclaimed.

"Not really a ballroom, of course," Roger explained. "This is our formal banquet room. We just pushed the tables out of the way."

"Perfect," Beatrice replied.

Leigh looked down his nose. "My best friend in London is the nephew of a duke. His mansion has a real ballroom."

"Good for him," Roger replied sarcastically. "May I have the next dance, Miss Parker?"

His hopes soared when she agreed.

"Perhaps you could join the line at the refreshment table," he told the sulking cousin, as he took Beatrice's hand and led her to the dance floor.

Bea would later look back on the first dance with Roger as the moment life changed forever. She wasn't a good dancer. The opportunity to dance rarely came along in Milton Abbas, and she'd never danced a waltz. Yet, she found herself in the arms of a capable dancer and all she had to do was follow his lead when his hand on the small of her back guided her across the floor. Her feet obeyed the gentle press of his thighs. It was exhilarating and magical.

They didn't exchange pleasantries. There was no need for words. Eyes and flared nostrils communicated a silent message. She was in love with this man and he loved her. The truth of it caused her heart to race. Her body heated when he smiled his crooked smile.

When, at the end of the set, he asked if he could seek her father's permission to court her, she had no hesitation in responding with a shy nod.

Her exhilaration banished all thought of Peter's assertion he had a chum whose uncle was a duke.

Chapter 17

Windfall

Bea fretted. A week had gone by and there was still no sign of Roger's promised visit. Had he changed his mind?

"He'll come," her father assured her as they ate breakfast. "It's a worrisome time for him with all that's going on."

She'd confided in him after he'd sensed her excitement, but she didn't want Peter to be privy to her secret. There'd be time enough to tell him once her relationship with Roger was confirmed as serious.

"Who are you expecting?" her cousin asked, with his mouth full of buttered toast.

"Sandiford," her father replied gleefully. "He wants to court Bea."

Furious he'd divulged her secret, Bea was nevertheless mystified by Peter's reaction. Scowling, he dropped the toast, threw down his napkin, and stood. "You can't marry a trades-man," he shouted, eyes narrowed and thunder darkening his face. "Your behavior with him at the wake was scandalous. Besides, I planned to ask for your hand again. I'm a much more suitable candidate. He's even been questioned about the murder of that unfortunate lad."

Bea's throat tightened. She hadn't known Roger had been a suspect, but it was a ridiculous notion. How had Peter become aware of it? She retorted without thinking. "But you're my cousin, Peter, on top of which I don't love you."

"What's love got to do with it?" he asked indignantly.

"If you have to ask that question, then you ..."

A demanding knock at the front door signaled a reprieve. Thinking Roger had come calling at last, she hurried into the foyer in time to see Glenda open the door.

"What are you doing here?" her maid demanded.

Bea stared in disappointed disbelief at a pair of bright yellow pantaloons.

The shocks continued when Peter nigh on knocked Glenda over and shook hands with the visitor, "James," he exclaimed. "What a nice surprise. How did you get here?"

"Peter," a grinning Odlum replied. "Bosom beau. Took a hack and the insolent driver was none too happy to bring me out to the back of beyond."

The penny dropped. Peter's pal with the ducal uncle was James Odlum, and Bea doubted very much if his visit was a surprise to Peter.

"Odlum," her father shouted gleefully when he entered the foyer. "Come in, come in."

Bea was wary. She'd never fully trusted Odlum, nor Peter for that matter, but her father had always appreciated the fop's help in getting them to Lancashire.

Arm in arm with his *bosom beau*, Peter led the way into the sitting room.

"I say," Odlum announced, as he made himself at home on the settee. "You've worked wonders with this place."

Bea wondered how he knew that, since he hadn't accompanied them on their first visit to Belmont Grange. Even her father raised an eyebrow.

"Peter told me what a ruin it was."

His statement didn't ease Bea's misgivings. Even Peter hadn't seen the original dilapidated state of the Grange, and when could the pair have discussed it?

"You're wondering why I'm here," the fop said, as he extracted a sheaf of papers from his satchel. "Messrs. Hardman, Burgesse, and Hilton sent me with this documentation. It was apparently overlooked. Some mix-up at the Westminster Bank."

Her father adjusted his spectacles as Odlum handed him the documents.

Bea worried when the color drained from his face. "I'm so sorry. This changes the future," he said.

It wasn't so much the words that bothered Bea as the fact they were addressed directly to her.

"THINGS ARE LOOKING UP," Roger told his mother as they sat down for breakfast. "Two payments received on overdue accounts this week."

He'd divulged nothing about Miss Parker's willingness to accept his courtship. Experience had taught him never to count his chickens before they hatched. Nevertheless, life ran more smoothly when a man was in love and the feelings were reciprocated.

"I wondered why you seem chipper these days," Lucinda replied. "I thought perhaps there was news of progress with the investigation."

"No, although Halliwell and I visited Mrs. Pickering. Did you know she has ten children?"

"Did she say if her son came home after work that day?"

"No, he didn't, but she mentioned he rarely does. Apparently, he and a couple of *delinquents* hang about the mill getting into mischief."

"Did she give you names?"

"No. To be honest, she seemed relieved to have one less mouth to feed."

His mother narrowed her eyes, a sure sign he had to offer a better excuse for his good humor. "Well, Brownlow's bales have the mules humming again, if only for a short time."

"That's not the reason," she insisted. "I watched you and Miss Parker at the ball last week. You're smitten with her."

She knew him too well, and Roger couldn't contain himself. "Be happy for me, Mama. She's agreed to accept my suit. I planned to seek her father's permission before now, but getting the mill running again has kept me busy."

"You know what they say. Strike while the iron is hot."

"I'll go out to the Grange this very day," he declared, suddenly panicked by the possibility Beatrice might have changed her mind.

"I hope you've thought this through," Lucinda cautioned.

"There's nothing to think about," he replied.

"I suppose I always assumed you'd wed a Lancashire lass. You have nothing in common with Beatrice Parker."

"Except that we love each other."

"Only time will tell," Lucinda sighed.

"I don't understand," Bea replied to her father's statement.

"It's a mortgage," he explained. "On Sandiford's mill."

"It appears the late baron held the mortgages on Broadclough Mill and the Sandiford dwelling," Odlum supplied. "Now, his heir holds them."

"But what does that mean?" Bea asked, dread knotting her innards.

"It means," her father said slowly, "if Sandiford defaults, I'll have no choice but to repossess the mill and the house."

"Exactly," Odlum replied, with too much glee for Bea's liking. "Apparently, contrary to expectations, he's managed to scrape together the latest payment, and I have it here, minus our commission of course. It seems the late baron didn't trust the bank. He always demanded the cash be brought to him."

Her suspicions mounting, Bea watched Odlum count out four five-pound notes into her father's hand.

Her father stared at the money. It was more than he earned in a year in Milton Abbas. Surely this financial windfall meant a brighter future. If her father held the mortgage, Roger need never worry about ...

"In light of this development," her father said wearily. "I cannot give my blessing to Sandiford's suit. And he must never know I hold the mortgages."

"But Papa," she wailed.

Peter patted her hand. "You must understand, my dear," he said with a patronizing grin. "Business and pleasure don't mix."

As HE STEPPED DOWN from his brougham, Roger was pleased to note the immense improvement in the gardens surrounding Belmont Grange. The dead trees and shrubs had been removed and the weeds banished. Even the house looked less like a gothic ruin.

Approaching the door, he mused about moving Beatrice into his home once they married. It wouldn't be easy with Lucinda, but surely his mother would see he loved Beatrice and make allowances. He hoped Miss Parker hadn't become too attached to the Grange. It was a nonsensical thought. She hadn't lived on the moor long enough to ...

His thoughts were interrupted when the unwelcome cousin emerged from the house in the company of a fellow who could only be the ponce he'd met briefly at the train station. As far as he was aware, no one else wore bright yellow pantaloons. The pair were giggling like schoolboys. An elusive memory nagged at him but Leigh spoke before he could gather his thoughts.

"Sorry, old chap," the Londoner crooned. "My uncle wanted me to convey his regrets. Beatrice is already spoken for."

"Spoken for?" Roger echoed, fearing he was hallucinating.

"She and I are betrothed," came the reply.

"I see," Roger muttered, afraid his trembling legs might buckle. He had to get back to the carriage with his shattered pride intact. Beatrice had led him on when all the while she'd known she was promised to another. Peter had been laughing at him.

Chapter 18

Up To No Good

Having taken refuge in her bedroom, Bea gripped the windowsill and watched Roger stalk back to his carriage without a backward glance. Peter and his foppish friend followed the brougham down the track a little way. They turned back to the house, arms around each other's shoulders, grinning like schoolboys.

"Bosom beaux, indeed," she hissed.

Something untoward was going on, but she couldn't put her finger on what it might be.

The news of her father's windfall was too much to process. It appeared this new-found source of income meant the end of her hopes for a relationship with Roger. Her father seemed adamant. If only Roger had come into the house, she might have explained. They could have discussed it rationally, though she was completely out of her depth as far as business dealings went. Whatever her cousin said to him had resulted in a hasty retreat. The prospect of losing Roger tightened her throat. The tears followed unbidden.

~

ROGER MIGHT HAVE KNOWN his newly married sister would be visiting when he got home. His face must have betrayed his anguish.

"Things not going well with Miss Parker?" Philippa cooed.

"Mind your own business," he retorted.

"Leave him be," his mother commanded.

His gloating sister lifted her chin and floated out of the drawing room.

"Tell me," Lucinda said softly.

How to confess that Beatrice had broken his heart? "She's promised to another," he growled.

Lucinda cocked her head to one side. "That cannot be," she replied at last. "Who can have courted her?"

"Her cousin, Peter Leigh."

"Nonsense. I could tell at the ball that she doesn't even like him. He's not suitable for the likes of Beatrice Parker."

"Neither am I, apparently."

"She told you this?"

"No, Peter told me."

"And you believe him?"

Now that an icy calm had loosened the knot in his belly, Roger recalled the curious presence of the fop. Odlum was his name, according to Arthur Parker's accounts of the journey. Why was he at Belmont Grange? He was very friendly with Peter Leigh. What were the two of them up to?

BEA WASN'T sure how long she'd lain with her face buried in the pillow. She'd cried until her throat was dry and her nose completely stuffed up. Wearily, she turned her head and opened her eyes, taken aback to see Glenda sitting in the rocking chair beside her bed.

She sat up and blew her nose on the handkerchief her maid handed over.

"Don't worry," Glenda said. "It'll all work out with Mr. Sandiford."

"How can it work out?" she replied hoarsely. "Papa seems adamant."

"Pshaw. The mortgages are the least of yer concerns."

"I don't understand."

"You mark my words, that cousin of yours and Odlum are up to something."

Bea wasn't surprised by the accusation. Glenda had resented Odlum since the journey from Dorset and the unfortunate incident at the Hotel Victoria. "You've never liked the lawyer's clerk."

"That's beside the point. You didn't like him either."

"I have to admit you're right. Still."

"Did ye know Leigh and Odlum are close friends?"

"Not until he showed up here."

"Does it perhaps explain why Peter came to the funeral?"

"What are you saying?"

"It's too much of a coincidence. I think Peter knew about the mortgages."

Bea began to see where this was going. "Odlum could easily have caused the delay in notifying us."

"Exactly, and now, the two of them are downstairs putting all kinds of ideas into your poor papa's head."

Bea acknowledged her father hadn't been himself since his wife's death. "Ideas?"

"They're pressing for Peter to wed ye."

The fog cleared. Roger had left because he thought ... "They told Mr. Sandiford I was promised to Peter."

"I think ye're right. And they've planted the notion the late Baron Belmont must have hoarded the money in the house."

Bea had to admit that made sense. "He didn't trust banks, and lived here as a recluse."

"Now, miss, we must find that money before the pair downstairs get their greedy hands on it."

"Finally, dear Glenda," Bea exclaimed. "Your eavesdropping has borne fruit."

AGAINST HIS BETTER JUDGEMENT, Roger sent the brougham to pick up Miss Parker the day after he'd been humiliated once again. The lessons had to continue. Fool that he was, he couldn't abide the thought of Beatrice traveling in the late baron's decrepit carriage. The Belmont stables were empty in any case. "I suppose the old fool was too miserly to get rid of the carriage or buy a horse," he muttered to himself, determined to avoid running into the woman who'd broken his heart. He'd have to stay out of his study for a while. Her lingering scent would be too much to bear.

Taking refuge in his bedroom when he heard the crunch of the brougham's wheels in the yard, he cursed his weakness. He couldn't allow Beatrice Parker to turn him into a coward. He'd never shied away from a challenge and this should be no different, although he'd always kept his heart out of previous dealings.

After checking his neckcloth in the cheval mirror, he opened the door, took a deep breath and started down the stairs.

DESPERATE TO EXPLAIN to Roger that she had no intention of marrying Peter, Bea inquired as to his whereabouts as soon as she entered his home.

"I believe I saw Mr. Sandiford go upstairs a short while ago," Borden replied.

She hesitated. The bedrooms were upstairs. The upper floor was out of bounds for her, now she no longer resided in the house. In addition, she wasn't certain if explaining her unengaged status to Roger was the right thing to do, since her father had forbidden her to tell him about the mortgages. And it was apparently the financial benefit to her family that would deny her the chance at happiness with Roger.

Her courage deserted her when she suddenly realized she was halfway up the stairs and he was coming down. "I'm sorry," she cried, before turning tail and running for the study.

Fists clenched, Roger resisted the temptation to hurry after Miss Parker. Her students would think it odd if they both rushed into the study. What would he say if he did follow her? He could hardly berate her in front of his workers. And what was she doing climbing the stairs? Was she planning on making some excuse for leading him on? As if *I'm sorry* made everything all right.

Indecision and frustration combined to make his knees tremble. He sat down on the stairs, hating the weakling he'd become—all thanks to a woman. The invincible Roger Sandiford brought low by love.

Raking his hair back off his forehead, he resolved to get hold of his emotions. Never again would he allow a woman into his heart.

Chapter 19

Quandary

B ea had always prided herself on her ability to keep calm in any circumstances. However, as the Sandiford brougham carried her home after the classes, she admitted she'd never had to deal with challenges like the ones she faced now. The gaping students in her mathematics class must have thought she was having some sort of stuttering episode. She'd been on edge, half expecting a furious Roger to come charging into the study.

She tried to organize her chaotic thoughts. If the late baron had squirreled away the mortgage money, it was imperative she and Glenda find it before Peter and Odlum did. The difficulty lay in searching without her cousin realizing that's what they were doing.

And what of her papa? He seemed to think the new financial realities precluded a relationship between her and Roger. He claimed he'd have no choice but to repossess the mill and the house if Roger defaulted. That seemed ludicrous to her. What would they do with an unproductive mill? Would her father really toss Lucinda Sandiford out of her home? Had the windfall and his new title changed him so much? Or perhaps his wife's death had stolen more of his wits than she realized.

Wouldn't a true Christian be willing to carry Broadclough Mills until the American war was over? They'd survived before without the income from Roger's payments.

If her father insisted she marry Peter against her will, then he really had changed. She refused to accept that.

Preoccupied with her thoughts, she didn't notice the rain had started until the carriage halted in front of the Grange. She might have known. The skies had a habit of clouding over as soon as she reached the moors.

The inclement weather matched her mood.

As usual, the driver climbed down from his perch, opened the door and let down the steps. Efficient as ever, he opened a large umbrella. She paused, certain no one from the house would appear with an umbrella to protect her from the downpour.

Roger's driver walked her to the door, bowed and took his leave. It struck her he was more of a gentleman than either of the manipulative pair in the house.

She'd accused Roger of not being a gentleman. She now realized she hadn't known what a true gentleman was. Preconceived snobbish beliefs had cost her the man she loved. She feared her heart might break.

A red-faced Glenda hurried to greet her in the foyer. "I spent the afternoon searching in the attic," she whispered. "Nothing."

"Did Peter not get suspicious?"

"Told him it was high time we did something about the attic since the workers left it in a jumble of unwanted furniture."

"What did he and Odlum do while I was gone?"

"I'm not sure, but I heard cupboard doors banging and they're in the cellar at the moment."

"Papa too?"

"No. He's reading a book in the sitting room."

So, they hadn't involved her father in their search. That news brought a glimmer of hope. There might not be another opportunity to speak with him privately.

"You're missing your newspaper, Papa," she began, as she breezed into the sitting room.

"Yes," he agreed, closing his book. "A daily newspaper is a luxury I never had in Milton Abbas. I fear the time we spent with the Sandifords spoiled me."

"I suppose we'll get used to this place eventually."

Her father removed his spectacles. "I admit I'm not looking forward to living here alone when you marry."

Bea flopped down on the settee in an effort to appear nonchalant. "What makes you think I'll be moving away?"

"Well, my dear, Peter's a Londoner. He won't want to live here."

She realized the time for subtlety had passed. "I won't be marrying Peter. I don't trust him and I certainly don't love him."

"But ..."

She got to her feet. "If you had any love at all for my mother, you'll understand why I won't marry anyone if I can't marry Roger Sandiford."

She regretted the pain that contorted her father's face. She'd never in her life argued with him.

"You know that's out of the question now," he replied. "You've never liked Sandiford in any case."

Bea hadn't realized what a masterful performance of disdain she'd given. "You're wrong. I love Roger Sandiford. Why is it out of the question, Papa?" she retorted, feeling the heat rising in her face. "Is the money from the mortgages more important than my happiness? What on earth will you do with Roger's mill if you have to repossess it?"

"We'll sell it, of course," Peter said as he and Odlum entered the drawing room unexpectedly.

Taken by surprise and afraid they might have overheard too much, Bea swallowed the lump in her throat. It was as plain as the nose on her face what these two were up to, but she was outnumbered, and had been brought up never to question a man's authority. "Is that what you want, Papa? To ruin a man you respect?" she asked as she fled the room.

Roger retreated to the spinning room. Despite the heat, the noise, and the cotton dust, he'd always found it to be the place he did his best thinking. Brownlow's bales wouldn't last long, but at least the mill was producing again.

It was the persistent coughing that drew his attention to one of his workers—Bridget, the girl Beatrice had befriended, if he wasn't mistaken.

Miss Parker had more or less accused him of causing the girl's illness. Coughs were a fact of life in any mill, but Bridget's seemed particularly deep in her chest.

When the spinning mule came level with him, he took the opportunity to speak to her. "You're Bridget?" he asked.

She glanced at him for only a second, but he took note of the wariness in her eyes. "Aye, sir," she replied, before the mule advanced again, taking her away from him.

"Don't be nervous," he said, when the mule moved backwards again. "Miss Parker came to see you."

A smile lit her haggard face. "She did, Mr. Sandiford. Brought a basket."

Still coughing, she advanced with the mule.

"Thinks the world of you, she does," Bridget told him hoarsely when she reached him again.

It was obvious the girl was sick, yet she'd come to work. He didn't need to ask the reason. "Can no one at home take your place until you feel better?" he asked, walking forward with her as the machine advanced.

"I've a sister. Meg's over yonder on t'other mule. Da works at Hampson's."

He toyed with the idea of sending his mother's doctor to Bridget's home, but Richards would likely balk at venturing to Red Lane. He had a pathetic urge to question her further about her assertion Miss Parker held him in high esteem, but their conversation had already attracted too much attention. The master had taken the time to talk with a mill girl. Tongues would wag. Nodding, he walked off to another part of the mill.

But Bridget's claim set him thinking. If Miss Parker liked him, why had she rejected him in favor of her cousin? He'd been sure she didn't even like Peter Leigh. Had his unfailing instincts about people suddenly gone awry? Had the blow to his pride blinded him to what was really going on?

OBLIGED to travel into Bolton each day to keep up her work with the classes, Bea had no choice but to leave the searching up to Glenda. She'd been able to thoroughly search her own room, though she hadn't expected to find anything there. At least it could be crossed off the list.

She assumed Peter and Odlum had found nothing in the cellar since they continued to comb through every other room in the house.

"I'm beginning to think there is no hidden treasure," she whispered to the maid before leaving the morning after the argument with her father.

"So, what became of the money over the years?" Glenda asked. "He didn't spend it on the house, nor on wages to pay servants."

The quandary preoccupied her all the way into Bolton. It was imperative she and Glenda find the cache, if it existed. Peter only wanted to marry her so he'd have access to her father's income from the mortgages. He and Odlum would fritter away the funds. It seemed her father couldn't see he was being manipulated.

And she had to set things right with Roger. Make him understand this situation was none of her doing.

Of one thing she was certain. The unemployed workers needed the money more than she and her father did.

Chapter 20

Bridget

Hoping Brownlow's bales would provide at least a week's worth of work, Roger returned to the spinning room. He refused to admit he wanted to speak at greater length with Bridget, to find out more about her impression of Beatrice's feelings for him.

His gut tightened when he discovered another woman had taken her place. Something must be terribly wrong if she hadn't come to work. A few minutes later, thanks to being pointed in the right direction by other spinners, he located her sister. "Meg, isn't it?" he asked. "Where's Bridget?"

There was no mistaking the grief in her eyes. "She couldn't breathe this morning. I had to leave her."

His thoughts went to Beatrice. "Does Miss Parker know?"

"No, sir. I haven't seen her today."

"I'll make sure she's told," he replied, unwilling to contemplate the fate of a young woman left to suffer alone in a hovel.

Confident this was a day when the mathematics class was scheduled, he soon reached his study. Taking a deep breath, he forced himself to enter slowly. He didn't want to alarm Beatrice nor give the young workers something to gossip about.

His arrival caused a stir, but Beatrice's green eyes betrayed her as she came to greet him. She was glad to see him.

He inhaled her perfume as he whispered close to her ear, "Bridget hasn't come to work."

"I'll go at once," she replied, immediately understanding the implications.

"You cannot go alone. I'll accompany you."

"Very well," she said.

After she'd explained the urgency to the students, they were on their way within minutes. When she linked her arm with his, hope surged, prompting him to take a risk. He couldn't stick to his resolve to shut her out of his heart. "You belong on my arm, Beatrice," he said.

Her reply astounded him. "I know that. We just have to convince my father."

He suddenly didn't care that they were on a public street, in full view of passers-by. He took her into his embrace and kissed her.

Closing her eyes, Bea surrendered to the power of Roger's kiss. He nibbled her lips gently at first, then the kiss intensified as he groaned, coaxing her mouth open with his tongue. Delicious desires blossomed in secret places when his tongue delved into her mouth. It seemed natural to welcome the invasion with her own tongue. The taste of pure male was intoxicating. His subtle cologne stole up her nostrils.

He gathered her closer to his hard body, his arms gripping her tightly. Lost in the spell, she risked opening her eyes, dismayed to see they'd been encircled by a group of grinning youths. Apparently sensing her withdrawal, Roger broke off the kiss. His satisfied smile vanished when he saw the lads. "Have you never seen a man kiss a woman before?" he demanded, shielding her from their view. "Get about your business."

They ran off, laughing and whistling.

"We'll be the talk of the town," she lamented.

"Do you care?" he asked.

She wilted in the face of his intense gaze. "It's a complicated situation," she replied, realizing she wasn't answering his question.

"I love you, Beatrice. If you love me, it's not complicated at all."

She longed to explain, but her father had forbidden it. "Please, let's hurry to see Bridget," she pleaded, as she pulled away from him.

Jaw clenched, he nodded. "You do love me, Beatrice and I'm not giving up without a fight," he said.

Hope warred with fear. She couldn't deny she loved him, but her cousin and his odious friend would fight him tooth and nail. Who knew what the pair was capable of?

She accepted his arm and they set off once more for Red Lane.

It wasn't the first time Roger had entered the home of one of his workers, but he'd never seen such a dank hovel as Bridget's dwelling. The cellar brought back too many dark memories he'd sooner forget. The windowless place reeked of tobacco and human waste. The walls were black. Eyes closed, the girl lay in a box bed in one corner. Her chest rose and fell, making an eerie wheezing sound that filled the room.

A man slumped in a rocking chair, sucking on a pipe. Roger wrinkled his nose as clouds of acrid blue smoke stole up his nostrils.

"Her father," Beatrice explained. "Mr. Mann."

Roger yanked the pipe out of the man's mouth and threw it into the street. "Get out of here," he growled.

Mann leaped to his feet, fists clenched, his nose inches from Roger's, but he seemed to quickly lose his courage. He backed away and slunk out of the house without a word.

Roger left the door open for fresh air to dissipate the smoke. "How is she?" he asked, humbled to realize he'd never concerned himself with the health of any particular worker. Beatrice had forced him to see his workforce as human beings and not just a means to an end.

"Not good," she whispered. "I watched my mother's lungs lose the battle in the struggle for air. This sounds the same."

They kept vigil for what seemed like hours, Beatrice holding Bridget's hand, Roger in the chair Mann had vacated. Strangely, it felt right to be with the woman he loved while she tended a dying girl, promising to look after Meg.

"She's gone," Beatrice finally rasped when the wheezing stopped. "No more pain."

Roger took her into his arms and rocked her while she sobbed. "I'm sorry," he said, though the words seemed inadequate.

"I'm not sure what to do next," she said.

"I'll fetch the undertaker," he replied. "Will you be all right here alone for a little while?"

She nodded and he was about to leave when Mann staggered into the hovel. Red-rimmed eyes betrayed his grief. He went straight to the bed where Bridget lay, gathered her into his arms, and wept.

"Go," Beatrice urged Roger when he hesitated. "He won't harm me."

"I'll see to the funeral," Roger told Bridget's father.

"Least tha can do," Mann hissed between gritted teeth.

Chapter 21

Confrontation

B ea supposed that her previous life in Dorset had insulated her from the harsh realities of life. A vicar's daughter had little to do with farm laborers and the like who perhaps endured poor working conditions and died cruel deaths in primitive hovels.

However, Bridget's suffering brought home to her the necessity for change in the industrial heartland of her country. As a woman alone, she could do very little, but with money came influence. It was more vital than ever that she find the late baron's hidden funds. They'd ascertained from the bank that he hadn't deposited the money. It made sense that he had stashed the cash in the house—but where?

She also had to find some way to change her father's mind about Roger. She resolved to speak to him after Bridget's funeral.

One bright spot in all the sorrow was a reply from Edith. Bea was thrilled to learn her friend was happy and the new mother of a baby girl, but the news only increased her longing for Roger Sandiford and a family of her own. Edith's commiserations about Bea's unhappiness with Lancashire and her lengthy descriptions of local gossip opened her eyes. She realized to her own amazement she had no desire to return to Dorset.

LEGS BRACED, Roger stood in a different cemetery, but the east wind was just as bitingly cold as it had been on that day not so long ago when Abigail Parker was buried.

This time, he was the one supporting Beatrice as Bridget Mann's coffin was lowered into the grave. There was no sign of Peter Leigh and his foppish friend.

Apart from Arthur Parker and the minister, Bridget's father and younger sister were the only other mourners on the windswept hillside. Apparently recovered from his anger, Mann had thanked Roger profusely for covering the funeral expenses. Roger wished the fellow had held on to some of his outrage over his daughter's death. He'd previously decided against installing better ventilation in his mill. Now, it would be a priority—if he didn't lose Broadclough to his creditors.

When Beatrice walked over to express her condolences to Bridget's family, Roger took the opportunity to turn to Arthur Parker. "I would venture a guess that this burial has dragged up terrible memories," he said.

"Yes," Arthur replied, his gaze fixed somewhere in the far distance.

"May I ask, sir, why you've turned against me?"

Arthur swiveled his head to look at him. "Turn against you? My dear fellow ..."

"You can't deny you've forbidden any relationship between me and your daughter, and I would know the reason."

Swaying on his feet, Arthur paled.

"I love her," Roger said. "If you doubt that ..."

Parker held up his hand. "No. I'm sure ... er ... I had resolved not to tell you this but, if I do, you will understand my motives."

"Tell me what?"

"The late baron held the mortgages on your mill and your home. They've devolved to me."

"The wily old fox!" Roger exclaimed. "I never knew. His lawyers arranged the financing. But why does this prevent me from marrying your daughter?"

"Because I'll assign the mortgages to her when I pass on. She must have income, and she cannot inherit the barony."

"But her son could," Roger replied.

"Which is the reason she must marry Peter before much more time elapses."

"I will never marry Peter," Beatrice declared as she returned to her father's side. "I know you always think everyone's motives are honorable, but I don't trust Peter, nor his bosom beau."

Arthur frowned. Roger hoped he was finally seeing the obvious. "Does it not strike you as suspicious that Peter is Odlum's best friend?" he asked. "The fop clerks for the late baron's law firm. He must have known about the mortgages."

"Were you not surprised when Peter showed up at the funeral?" Beatrice asked.

"I suppose I was," Arthur confessed. "I admit I wasn't thinking clearly."

"It was a trying time," Beatrice agreed. "But my cousin doesn't love me. I think he is after your income from the mortgages, Papa."

"And your barony, sir," Roger added. "If he succeeds in fathering a son on Beatrice ..."

Arthur rubbed his whiskers. "You might be right, now I think on it. He always was a selfish child."

"So, I have your blessing to court Beatrice?" Roger asked, extending a hand.

"You do," Arthur replied, returning the handshake.

A cemetery wasn't the appropriate place for Roger to kiss his beloved, especially when they were standing beside a newly dug grave, but he didn't care. He put his arm around her waist and bestowed a chaste peck on her cheek. "I promise to spend my life making your daughter happy."

Bridget's family joined them and together everyone proceeded out of the cemetery. Roger acknowledged Meg's curious wink with a tip of his hat.

STILL FLOATING on air now that her father had given permission for Roger to court her, Bea agreed with his opinion that Roger not accompany them back to Belmont Grange. The plan was to inform Peter and Odlum that there would be no marriage between the cousins. The Londoners were unpredictable and Roger's presence might result in fisticuffs.

"We should have confided in Roger about the hidden money," she told her father, as they traveled across the moor in the Sandiford brougham.

"It might not even exist," he replied.

"I am convinced it does. Think of what we could achieve with that money."

"I suspect spending it on yourself isn't what you have in mind."

"We both know it should fund more relief for the workers, and perhaps some on the house."

"You put me to shame, young lady. All I could see was the security it would bring you if we put it in the bank."

"Where it would do no one any good. Roger is my security.

He'll weather this setback in his fortunes. That's the kind of man he is."

He patted her hand. "Can you forgive a foolish old man for not seeing the obvious?"

"You were grieving. There's nothing to forgive."

Chapter 22

Horses

After his driver dropped him off at home, Roger sought out his mother and shared his good news.

"I hope you know what you're doing," Lucinda replied grumpily, bringing the rocking chair to a halt.

Her jealous pout didn't surprise him. "Be happy for me. I love her and she loves me."

"She'll never love you as much as I do."

Roger didn't fault his mother. They'd weathered so many ups and downs together over the years. He kissed her forehead. "A mother's love is a precious thing," he agreed. "And I thank you for it."

"There's something else you're not telling me," she said.

He dithered, unsure how she would take the news about the mortgages. "Just that a man must move on and start a family of his own."

She narrowed her eyes, obviously not satisfied.

"The late Baron Belmont held the mortgages," he revealed. "Beatrice's father has inherited them."

Her eyes widened. "Who told you this?"

"Parker himself."

She drew her shawl around her shoulders and resumed rocking. He recognized the significance of her arched eyebrow. "Which begs the question," she said finally. "If you've been paying the late baron all these years, what did he do with the money?"

Roger shrugged. "Banked it, I suppose."

"Seems to me it was well known he didn't trust banks."

"And he certainly didn't spend it on the upkeep of the house."

An uneasy feeling began to percolate in Roger's gut. He trusted Peter Leigh and his chum even less now he knew there might be money stashed in the house. He'd thought they were chasing future income and the noble title, but perhaps there was more to their schemes. His mill was possibly at greater risk than he thought. If Peter got control of the mortgages and Roger defaulted, the fop and his pal would sell the buildings without a second thought.

They wouldn't take kindly to being told Beatrice was going to marry someone else.

WHEN THE SANDIFORD BROUGHAM halted in front of the Grange, Bea was astonished to see Peter and Odlum harnessing a horse to the dilapidated Belmont carriage. She was surprised they'd managed to move the old carriage out of the barn without it falling apart. As far as she knew, the estate owned no horses and she'd never seen this particular animal before. Its head drooped and its ribs stuck out of its skinny frame.

"What ho, Uncle," Peter called as he waved. "No further need to borrow a stranger's brougham. James and I bought Lightning here from a horse dealer so you can travel in your own carriage."

Bea privately thought they'd probably taken the pathetic creature off the knacker's hands. The nag was aptly named. It looked like it had been struck by lightning. As for pulling a carriage ...

"A word, Peter," her father said sternly after stepping out of the brougham.

Bea's cousin hesitated as his smile faded. He'd clearly detected a note of censure in the command. "I'll be with you in five minutes," he replied.

Glenda rushed to greet Bea and her father when they entered the house. "I have a terrible feeling those two miscreants have found the money," she whispered as she took their cloaks and hats. "They've been acting like giddy kippers all day."

"And they've bought a horse," Bea replied. "The animal and the carriage both look incapable of traveling a mile on an open road, never mind over moorland."

"They spent all morning messing about with that poor excuse for a carriage. Then they disappeared and came back riding the nag. They've either found the money or lost their wits."

"This doesn't bode well for what we have to tell them," her father said. "Peter's not going to take no for an answer."

"It might almost be better if they ride away with the money," Bea suggested.

Her father shook his head. "If Sandiford is right, they have their sights set on more than the money."

They waited in the drawing room. Hands clasped on her lap, Bea perched on the settee. Her father stood by the cold hearth. Informing her cousin that she intended to marry Roger suddenly loomed like a daunting task that might have ramifications she hadn't foreseen. She wished her champion had come with them.

145

MARCUS DECIDED to visit *The Pack Horse* after all. It wouldn't hurt to verify Mr. Leigh's statement about when he'd arrived in Bolton. Impatient to be on his way, he paid no mind to the urchin hanging about the mill yard.

"There's no food for you here," he told the lad, bothered by the fear in his eyes. "Go to the soup kitchen."

The boy shook his head. "Hafta speak with thee, Cunstable."

"I'm on my way into town," he replied.

"It's about Malcolm Pickerin' and the night he were kilt."

Marcus thought it was probably a waste of time to linger but, if the lad had information about the murder ... "Go on, but it had better be good."

"I'm Robbie Draper. Malcolm were me best pal."

The boy startled, his eyes darting here and there when a group of men wandered through the yard on their way to the soup kitchen. Suddenly recalling what Mrs. Pickering had said about her son's *delinquent* pals, Marcus feared the boy might bolt. "No need to be afraid. What can you tell me? I won't be angry."

"Me and Malcolm, we sometimes 'id int' mill after t' shift."

Marcus had an inkling what it was they got up to. Despite all the dire warnings about fire, the overseer had reported often finding fag ends in the spinning room of a morning. "You were smoking," he said.

Robbie studied his feet. "Aye, sorry Cunstable."

Marcus tapped the stripes on his sleeve. "I'm a sergeant, but go on."

"We were laughin' but we shut our gobs and docked the fags when we 'eard somebody comin'. We crawled into a dark corner when two men crept in. They were carryin' what looked like 'ammers or crowbars."

Marcus' hopes rose. There had been outsiders in the mill that night. "Machine breakers."

"Tha'da thought so, except fer their togs."

"What do you mean?"

"Well, I legged it, but they looked like gentlemen to me, and one wore the daftest yellow trousers I e'er seen."

Marcus tucked away that bit of information. It might prove useful. "You left Pickering in the mill?"

Robbie sniffled. "I thought he were right be'ind me, but they must ha' caught 'im."

Marcus ought to remonstrate with the lad. Why hadn't he come forward before? But he knew the answer and there was no time to lose. As he'd suspected, complete strangers might have murdered Malcolm Pickering.

CURSING himself for allowing Beatrice and her father to face Peter and his chum alone, Roger struggled with a dilemma. His two best horses, the matched grays, were harnessed to the brougham which hadn't yet returned from Belmont Grange. His mother had a pony to pull her gig, but she'd apparently gone visiting—something she rarely did.

The only horse remaining in the stables was Midnight, an unpredictable devil of a beast with a vicious mind of its own. After the first flush of success in the cotton trade, he'd fancied he should take up gentlemanly pursuits, like riding. He'd soon discovered he was no rider, and Midnight was determined to throw off anyone who tried to mount him. He'd avoided the animal ever since. But he had no choice.

Luckily, the ostler who took care of his horses was still in the stables, but Albert shook his head when Roger asked him to saddle the black beast. "Ah don't think tha ought to be on that 'oss. 'E's a right mardy bugger."

"Nevertheless, my business is urgent," Roger replied, though he shared Albert's opinion.

"Do what tha likes then!" Albert retorted. "Ah'll say nowt else."

Midnight snorted and stamped his feet while the experienced ostler struggled to get the saddle on him. Roger tried desperately to convince himself there really was no need to risk life and limb. Surely Beatrice and her father could handle Peter.

But he would never forgive himself if something untoward happened.

He was distracted by the breathless arrival of Sergeant Halliwell. Apparently equally surprised, Midnight chose the moment to kick the walls of his stall, resulting in a stream of colorful language from the ostler.

"I must speak with you," the policeman said.

"Can't stop to chat," Roger replied. "I believe Miss Parker is in danger."

"From whom?" Halliwell asked.

"Her cousin and his foppish friend. I'm riding out to the Grange."

"I'll get the force out to assist, but I came to tell you I know who the killers are. At least, I've learned they were two men dressed like gentlemen and one wore yellow trousers."

The revelation was like a blow to the belly. It was the fop he'd seen in the street and Peter was his companion. "That's Odlum, the cousin's chum."

"You go on," Halliwell urged. "I'll get men out to the Grange and arrest the pair."

His gut in knots, Roger could only nod.

Albert dragged the reluctant horse into the yard and

boosted Roger into the saddle, muttering under his breath about foolish masters.

At first the horse shook his head and refused to move, despite Roger's frantic efforts with the stirrups.

"Beatrice is depending on us," he told Midnight, exasperated by the stubborn horse. "It'll be your fault if something bad happens at Belmont Grange."

Suddenly, they were off, bolting out of the yard and down Turton Street, headed for Blackburn Road and the town center.

Chapter 23

Abduction

Bea was dismayed when Peter entered the sitting room. She might have known he'd bring his pal along. She'd taken a dislike to Odlum on the journey north. Now, she found him more than a little intimidating.

"You don't seem pleased with the horse," her cousin whined.

She'd hoped her father would open the conversation, but he gaped, seemingly as thrown off balance as she felt.

"We don't wish to discuss horses, do we Papa?" she tried.

"Er ... It's not that we're ungrateful," her father replied.

She clenched her fists. Odlum would take charge of the conversation if her father didn't put his foot down.

"Certainly seems that way," the fop said belligerently.

Thankfully, her father didn't back down. "We want to discuss Peter's marriage to Beatrice."

"Good, yes," Peter replied. "Three weeks is necessary for the banns to be read. I can't wait."

Bea couldn't allow the farce to go on. "I told you before, and I'll tell you again, Peter. I won't marry you."

Her cousin scowled and opened his mouth to retort, but Odlum put a restraining hand on his arm.

"That's that, then," James said. "Nothing more to be added. Come along, Peter."

They left the room without a backward glance.

Smiling his relief, her father slumped into a chair. "Well, that was easy."

"Too easy," she replied, as the knot of disquiet tightened in her belly.

~

As Midnight galloped along, Roger swore he'd never ride again if he got to the Grange in one piece. His hat flew off before he and the devil horse even left the cobblestone streets of the town center, but he didn't dare stop to retrieve it. The beast likely wouldn't have halted if Roger had tried to rein him in.

It was a good thing he'd worn gloves, else his hands would have frozen. As it was, he might never straighten his stiff fingers again. His jaw might remain permanently clenched.

They'd stayed on the right road, though that certainly wasn't thanks to any guidance Roger had provided. It was as if the horse knew where they were headed.

At the edge of the moor, he passed his brougham returning to town. His driver gaped as Roger galloped past, too much of a coward to raise a hand in salute.

The horse tossed his head but didn't slow as the terrain grew more rugged. Roger feared he might end up broken and bleeding in some moorland ditch, but it gradually dawned on him that Midnight was enjoying himself. Unfortunately, that didn't make the experience any less terrifying nor the chafing any less painful.

If he ever managed to stop the horse and dismount, it was doubtful his legs would keep him upright.

Feigning nonchalance, Bea watched over Glenda's shoulder while the maid whipped up the batter for scones.

"Patience," Glenda urged. "I thought you'd have grown out of wanting to scrape the bowl when I'm done."

"No," Bea teased. "In fact, it gets more enticing as time passes."

Glenda smiled indulgently. "If you don't let me get on, these scones won't be ready for luncheon."

When the baking was in the oven of the ancient wood stove, Glenda handed the bowl to Bea. Using a spoon, she scooped out the remaining batter clinging to the sides.

"Delicious," she declared, popping the bowl in the sink when there was no more batter to eat. "I'll get the men to come to the table."

"Yer cousin's still outside playing with his new toy."

Sucking the sticky sweetness from her fingers, Bea wandered outside, hailing the visitors. "Luncheon's nearly ready," she called, absently wondering why the decrepit horse was still harnessed to the carriage. "Glenda baked scones."

"My favorite," Peter replied. "Don't you want to see how we've fixed up this old thing?"

She looked back at the house. "Perhaps after luncheon."

"It will only take a minute," he insisted.

Against her better judgement, she strolled over to inspect the exterior of the ancient conveyance. As far as she could tell, it looked no different from before. "Are you planning to refurbish the outside?" she asked.

"All in good time," Peter replied. "The interior is where you'll see a big difference."

"Probably not," she replied. "I've never been inside."

"All the more reason to look," he said. He opened the creaky door and climbed inside.

Joining him would be completely inappropriate, but Odlum stood right at her back. "I don't think..." she began.

Without warning, she was shoved into the musty-smelling carriage and landed in Peter's arms. She struggled to free herself when Odlum slammed the door, but her cousin held firm.

"What are you doing?" she demanded, as the carriage rocked. Fear closed her throat. Odlum had climbed into the driver's seat.

"Taking you to Gretna, my sweet," her cousin replied when the carriage lurched forward.

When she made to protest, he covered her nose and mouth with a rag. She inhaled a sickly aroma and quickly surrendered to dizzy oblivion.

ROGER FINALLY REACHED Belmont Grange without injury, but when Midnight came to a screeching halt, his breathless relief was short-lived. Arthur was standing outside the house, consoling a weeping Glenda. He'd come too late. Something dire had happened to Beatrice.

Arthur hurried toward him. "They've taken Bea," he rasped. "It's all my fault for encouraging my nephew."

A question nagged at Roger. There were no horses at Belmont Grange. "How did they take her?"

"In the old carriage. They bought a horse, though it's a poor specimen. I should have sensed."

"Never mind that now," Roger said, his hopes renewed.

Midnight had galloped hard but should have enough left to catch up to the dilapidated vehicle. "Which direction did they go?"

"We don't know," Glenda wailed. "I came out looking for Miss Bea and they were gone."

Roger had to make a decision. Far to the south lay London, Peter's home town. To the north ... "Gretna!" he exclaimed, urging Midnight to set off again.

Wondering if he should have shared the new information about Leigh and Odlum's possible involvement in the murder, Roger decided he was glad he hadn't. Parker and the maid were distraught enough without being told Beatrice was in the clutches of killers.

Chapter 24

Wreck

B ea tried to drag open her eyes. Her head ached. She was being tossed in some sort of bone-jarring contraption, but the temptation to slip back into sleep was powerful.

Eventually, panic threatened as what had happened gradually seeped back into her memory. Peter intended to take her to Gretna. She would never willingly consent to marry him, but he and Odlum were devious. They'd devise some scheme to trick her and the famous blacksmith.

It came to her she was sitting on the splintered floor, her hands tied, her back pressed up against the seat. Bracing her feet against the turbulent movement, she risked opening one eye. Peter dozed in a corner of the carriage, his hand on a lockbox. It appeared Glenda's assumption was correct. They'd found the money hidden in the old vehicle.

Given the pace Odlum had set, it was a miracle the carriage was still in one piece. It creaked and rattled. She wasn't sure how long she'd been asleep, and the windows were covered with old pieces of oilcloth. However, it was fairly dark within the conveyance. Surely, they didn't intend to drive all night?

The need for such breakneck speed was puzzling. No one

was coming in pursuit. The prospect of never seeing Roger again nigh on choked her.

"Good lad," Roger shouted when the old carriage came in sight, traveling at speed. Midnight tossed his head, confirming what Roger sensed. He and the horse had formed a bond. The feeling of euphoria was short-lived when a shot rang out. He'd been spotted. He pulled back, just far enough so he could keep the vehicle in sight. "We'll follow them all the way to Gretna if necessary," he declared, though he admitted inwardly that wouldn't be possible.

"But they're driving their nag hard," he said aloud, feeling somewhat silly talking to a horse. His spirits lifted. Glenda had said the kidnappers had bought a poor excuse for a horse. They'd be forced to call a halt for …

His heart stopped when he suddenly lost sight of his quarry. The sound of splintering wood reached his ears. The piercing cry of a horse in pain rent the air. Midnight's ears twitched. Roger reined in his mount and proceeded slowly in the direction of the terrible cries, his gut clenching when he saw three wheels of the old carriage spinning in air, the stricken horse struggling in vain to free itself from the overturned conveyance.

There was no sound from the carriage, no cries for help. He vowed to kill the men responsible for Beatrice's gruesome death. Then he saw the yellow trousers and realized fate had saved him the trouble. Odlum's body lay at an odd angle in a nearby ditch, his head caved in by a huge boulder.

BEA DIDN'T KNOW where she found the strength in her legs, but she lunged for Peter when he fired a pistol out of the window. If someone was in pursuit, it could only be Roger, though she didn't understand how that was possible. Hampered by the rope binding her wrists, she wrestled with her cousin until he flung her away. Suddenly, there was a loud crack and all hell broke loose. At first, she thought he'd shot her, but they were both tossed about the carriage like corks in a maelstrom. A blow to the head knocked her senseless.

The screeching cries of a horse in pain dragged her out of the stupor. She was upside down, her legs in the air. Something heavy lay between her outstretched legs, making it difficult to breathe. Whatever it was moved—Peter!

"Much as I love having you beneath me," he rasped. "Lie still or I'll blast your brains out."

She froze, puzzled by his jerky movements and the rustle of paper. "What are you doing?" she asked.

"I've worked ... too hard ... to leave this here," he replied. "Wily old coot hid the money in the last place we thought to look."

It came to her there were bank notes scattered all over the ruined carriage. He was trying to stuff them back into the lockbox next to her head, all the while trapped in the wreckage of the overturned carriage. Bea couldn't help herself. The situation was too comical for words. She laughed out loud.

THE SOUND of laughter startled Roger. Believing nobody could have survived the wreck and dreading he might find Beatrice lying broken and bleeding, he'd dismounted and was dejectedly contemplating how to put the injured nag out of its misery. Midnight snorted and pawed the ground.

Buoyed by the possibility Beatrice had survived, Roger hurried to the overturned carriage, said a silent prayer and succeeded in yanking open the door after three attempts. He fell backwards into the ditch when Peter barreled out and knocked him over. A pistol thrust in his face advised restraint, so he raised his hands as Leigh scrambled to his feet, a lockbox tucked under his arm. The wretch limped away and eventually managed to mount Midnight, whereupon he rode off into the dusk.

Wishing Peter well of the devil horse, and more concerned with Beatrice, Roger got to his feet and peered in the open doorway.

It was tempting to laugh at the fierce blush that reddened the face of the woman he loved. Bare legs stuck up in the air sported daintily embroidered pantalets. He briefly wondered if what he'd heard was true. Female unmentionables were reported to be crotchless.

He shook his head in an effort to banish lascivious thoughts. She presented a delightfully decadent sight, petticoats askew in a nest of bank notes. But she was alive and in one piece apart from a gash on her temple. "Beatrice," he exclaimed. "My love."

"The wretch had two pistols," she replied, trying to straighten her skirts with bound hands. "Find it for goodness sake and put that poor animal out of its misery."

He leaned in, untied the rope binding her wrists and kissed her with all the love and relief in his heart. She cradled his face and returned the kiss, opening readily to his coaxing tongue.

The sound of an approaching vehicle broke them apart.

Chapter 25

Rescue

"Please don't let anyone else see me in such a dreadful state," Bea urged when Roger told her another carriage was stopping to investigate.

"I'll need their help to get you out," he replied, clearly trying to be serious. "But let's see what we can do about your skirts."

Despite her predicament, her body heated when Roger's hand came close to her thighs as he pulled down her errant skirts. The twinkle in his eyes promised even greater delights once they were married. "Pick up the notes first," she commanded in an effort to take her mind off the situation. "We don't want people ..."

Roger pressed a finger to her lips. "The money is the least of my worries. There'll be time enough for that once we get you out safely."

They startled when a shot rang out. The heart-wrenching cries of agony ceased abruptly.

"Thank goodness," she said. "That poor animal."

After greeting her politely and reassuring her they would do their best to free her in no time, two men swarmed over the carriage, trying to ascertain how best to extract her. Their wives

161

uttered words of encouragement from somewhere out of Bea's line of sight. Roger did his utmost to protect her from debris when the two good Samaritans levered off the damaged side of the vehicle. He crawled in beside her and shoved pieces of splintered wood off her belly. "Are you hurt?" he asked. "Can you move?"

"I feel bruised, and I think Peter's lockbox hit me on the head, but I'm otherwise all right," she replied. "Get me out of here."

~

Roger's heart soared when Beatrice snaked her arms round his neck. He lifted her out of the wreckage, guided as he stepped backwards over wreckage by the two men who'd helped to free her.

"Let's get her into our carriage," the taller of the two said. "We're the Barton brothers from Preston. It's fortunate we had just left home when we came across your accident. We can take her there forthwith."

"It's the wisest option," Roger told Beatrice, who nodded her agreement.

There wasn't room in the carriage for everyone, so Roger and one of the brothers volunteered to stay behind and wait for a ride. Beatrice pleaded with Roger not to leave her, but it was clear she was exhausted, and the women soon convinced her they wouldn't be apart long.

The Barton vehicle had just disappeared when Midnight came trotting into view. "Whoa, boy," Roger urged, grabbing the reins.

"Magnificent beast," the younger Barton declared.

"Aye. Got me here just in time," he replied, stroking the

panting horse's muzzle. "I can't believe he's found his way back."

"If he's yours, where has he been?"

There was no choice but to reveal the whole story of Peter and Odlum's treachery. "That's Odlum's body in the ditch," he said. "They kidnapped Beatrice, intending to take her to Gretna."

"Gretna? In that carriage?" Barton asked incredulously. "I'm surprised it got this far without falling apart, especially with such a pathetic creature pulling it."

"I also believe they were responsible for the death of a young lad in Bolton. Peter rode off on Midnight, so I suppose he has the rest of the money."

"Which I assume they stole."

"They did. It's a long story, but the money belonged to the late Baron Belmont. Beatrice's father inherited it."

"Well, let's gather up what remains of it inside the carriage and you can tell my brother the details when we get to his home in Preston. He's the Superintendent of the local detachment of the Lancashire Constabulary. He'll soon have this Peter chap rounded up and dealt with."

Thrilled by the fortuitous turn of events, Roger shook his companion's hand. "I'm Roger Sandiford and I thank you."

"Sandiford, eh? From Broadclough Mills?"

"Aye. You know it?"

"Of its fine reputation, and the relief work you're providing for workers at this difficult time in the cotton industry. My brother's had to deal with a number of nasty situations here when masters have done nothing to ease the sting of unemployment."

"We're doing what we can," Roger replied. "Beatrice and her father have helped enormously."

"Let's hope the Americans stop fighting soon. Do you

suppose your horse could convey us both to Preston once we've gathered the money?"

"Fingers crossed," he replied, stuffing bank notes into his pockets.

UNDER THE SUPERVISION of Mrs. Barton, an army of maids quickly stripped Bea of her tattered clothes, bathed and dressed her in a clean nightgown, and tucked her up in a cozy bed.

The maids tutted at length about the bruises forming just about everywhere on her body. "I'm beginning to feel them too," she admitted.

She'd told some of the story during the short journey in the carriage, but the Bartons hadn't pressed her, obviously sensitive to the fact she was at the end of her tether. She recalled Mr. Barton revealing that he was a policeman.

Worried about Roger, who'd been abandoned on the highway, she dozed fitfully until being awakened by an argument in the corridor. "What's going on?" she asked the maid keeping vigil at her bedside.

"The young man wants to see you, but the housekeeper thinks it would be inappropriate."

"Nonsense. He's my fiancé and he saved my life. I want to see him."

She bobbed a curtsey and conveyed the message to the people in the corridor. A few seconds later, Roger swept into the room and gathered her into his arms. Unable to contain the fear any longer, she wept uncontrollably.

BEA'S HEART-WRENCHING sobs shuddered through Roger. Anger still held him in its thrall. He'd come too close to losing the woman he loved. "Hush, my darling lass," he said softly as he stroked her hair. "I can't tell you how good it feels to hold you."

"I feel safe now you're here," she replied.

"I came straight from the stables once I was sure Midnight was taken care of. I couldn't wait to see you."

"Midnight?" she asked.

"He's a horse I've owned for a while, but never ridden. It's a long story but suffice it to say he helped me catch up to the carriage you were in. I was furious when Peter stole Midnight and rode off, but the horse came back when Barton and I were waiting on the highway. We rode him here."

"So, we don't know where Peter is?"

"No, but Barton is the Superintendent hereabouts and he assures me men are already out looking for him. He's also sent word to Belmont Grange and my mother. I hate to tell you this, but it's possible they murdered Malcolm Pickering."

"How can that be? They weren't in Bolton then."

"As far as we know," he replied, not surprised when she remained silent for a few minutes. A killer in the family was a daunting prospect.

"I didn't know you are a rider," she said, obviously not wishing to pursue the matter.

"I'm not."

She cupped his face. "But you were determined to save me and I love you all the more for it."

She pursed her lips, inviting his kiss.

Their tongues mated, conveying the intense relief they both felt. It seemed natural to cup her breast. Her moan of pleasure echoed in his male parts, auguring well for future delights. He took a chance and brushed his thumb over her nipple, rewarded by a growl as she suckled his tongue.

"Don't stop," she whispered when they broke apart for breath. "I need ..."

Roger knew what she needed. "Would you like a little taste of the delights we'll enjoy in our marriage bed?"

When she nodded shyly, Roger slowly pulled up her nightgown and let his hand wander to the soft curls at the juncture of her thighs. "Once we do this, you're mine forever," he said, looking into her eyes.

"I want to be yours," she breathed in reply.

He bent his head to suckle a nipple through the fine fabric of her nightgown, then touched his finger to the diamond of her desire.

"I'm so wet," she lamented, opening her legs.

"Wet is good," he assured her, struggling to ignore the urging of his cock.

It took only a few strokes to bring her to completion. He smothered her cries of ecstasy with his kiss. "You are beautiful," he said, as she lay sated in his arms. "You can scream all you want to in our own bed, but we don't want to attract the censure of the Bartons' housekeeper."

"No," she agreed. "We owe this family a great deal."

"I should go. The servants are running a much-needed bath for me."

She nodded sleepily as he extricated himself from her embrace. It wouldn't take long for her to fall asleep. Tired but well-pleased with himself, he inhaled her essence on his fingers, growling as he left to seek his chamber.

Chapter 26

Aftermath

Despite the trauma of the crime committed against her, Bea slept well. Roger had introduced her to a brand-new world full of promise. The horror of Peter's betrayal and her duel with death had been banished by the prospect of a future with a loving husband who knew how to bring her to sexual rapture. Roger had awakened the woman within.

She wrestled with a dilemma. She longed to rise and find Roger. On the other hand, she wanted to lie abed, luxuriating in crisp, clean linens—and perhaps investigate the sensitive part of her most private place she hadn't known existed—wicked!

She stretched, feeling again the pulsing need deep within that she'd experienced last night.

A tap at the door heralded the maid, arms full of clothing. Wickedness had to be postponed.

"Tha's awake, I see," the smiling servant said.

"Yes, and I apologize that I've forgotten your name."

"I'm nay surprised after what tha went through yestereve. It's Emily, miss, and I've brung fresh togs. Th' lass what does washin' is sortin' yer things."

"That's kind, but not really necessary."

"If tha's a mind, the family's asked thee to join 'em for a late breakfast. Mr. Sandiford's there already."

The decision was easy. She longed to see Roger again. "I'm famished. Breakfast sounds good."

"Aye, I'm sure food's the reason tha's out o' bed sharpish," Emily teased.

THE MEN ROSE AS SOON as Beatrice entered the breakfast nook. She bestowed an arousing smile on Roger when he took hold of her hand. She looked remarkably well for a woman who'd undergone a terrifying ordeal. He wondered if anyone else saw what he saw on her face—the look of a woman who'd shared her first intimate interlude with a man.

He wanted to beat his chest and smugly proclaim to the world he was that fortunate man.

"All things considered, you're looking well, my lady," Thaddeus Barton declared. "I trust you slept well."

"I did," Beatrice replied.

Did the Bartons suspect the reason for her blush? "By the way, I'm not a lady," she said as Roger held out her chair.

"I understood from Mr. Sandiford that you're the daughter of the new Baron Belmont."

"Yes, but I've been Beatrice or Miss Parker all my life."

"As you wish," Mrs. Barton replied.

"We cannot thank you enough for your help," Roger told them. "We might still have been stranded had you not come along."

"That's doubtful," Barton replied. "It's a fairly well-traveled highway."

"Well, it's our good fortune it was you who came to our

rescue," Beatrice said. "And that you were able to put that poor horse out of its misery."

"Glad we could be of help," Barton replied. "My men have taken Odlum's body to the mortuary. Let's hope we soon have news of your cousin and the missing money, Miss Parker."

"Retrieving the money would be a bonus," Roger said. "I'm just relieved Beatrice wasn't seriously injured."

"Just a few cuts and bruises," she agreed. "Should we inform Odlum's employer of his death? He was a clerk for my father's new solicitors."

"I'll take care of that as soon as I have the details," Barton replied. "And I'll be in touch with the sergeant from Bolton regarding the new information about the murder at your mill."

"I'm glad you two will have your happily-ever-after," Mrs. Barton remarked. "It's plain to see you were made for each other."

"Thank you," Roger replied, quite certain Mrs. Barton sensed he and Beatrice had shared intimacies.

THERE WAS discussion at the breakfast table about Roger and Bea's return to Bolton. The Bartons apologized that their carriage was unavailable. "Beatrice and I can't ride Midnight," Roger said.

"You could ride home alone and send your carriage back for Miss Parker on the morrow," Mrs. Barton suggested.

Bea didn't want to be separated for Roger for even a day, but it would be rude to say so in front of their hosts. "I've yet to meet this horse that carried you to my rescue," she said. "Will you show him to me?"

"Of course," Roger replied, rising to assist Bea with her chair. "If our hosts don't mind."

"You young people go off and enjoy yourselves," Barton said. "I intend to see how the search is progressing. We'll work something out with regard to transport to Bolton."

Wishing they could, in fact, go off and *enjoy themselves*, Bea took Roger's arm, clinging to him as they made their way to the back door of the kitchen, across the windy yard and into the stable.

"I love the feel of your breasts pressed against my arm," he said close to her ear.

This new, intimate aspect of their relationship was secretly thrilling. "You're making me blush," she replied.

Extricating her arm from his, he narrowed his eyes, making her nipples tingle when he cupped her breasts. "I'd like to know if these beauties blush too."

"You're naughty," she retorted with a grin.

"And you like it."

"I do," she admitted, surrendering to his kiss when his lips met hers.

"'ow do," a gruff voice interrupted. "Hast come to see yon bugger of an 'oss?"

"GILBERT!" Roger exclaimed, irritated the elderly ostler had interrupted the kiss. Then he chuckled inwardly. He'd never before been caught in a compromising position—too rigidly strict with himself—until Beatrice. "Has he given any trouble?"

"Trouble's 'is middle name," Gilbert replied, removing his cloth cap and scratching his bald head as he led them to Midnight's stall. "Wants to be out gallopin'."

Beatrice pulled back when she saw the huge horse. "You rode that beast?" she asked.

"I had no choice," he replied, relieved when Midnight

allowed him to stroke his nose. "Seems he remembers our frantic ride."

He didn't blame her for keeping her distance. He could scarcely believe he'd ridden the black devil. "This is the young lady you helped me rescue," he told Midnight. "Her name's Beatrice. She's going to be my wife."

The horse eyed Beatrice.

"He's trying to decide if he likes me," she said, coming a little closer.

They both laughed when Midnight nudged her shoulder, but he shied away, snorting when the sound of carriage wheels on gravel disturbed the heart-warming scene.

Surprised to hear his mother's voice, Roger hurried to the door just in time to see Arthur Parker and Glenda alight from his brougham. "We're in here," he called when Lucinda marched toward the house.

He might have expected both parents would come as soon as they heard what had happened, but their arrival sounded the death knell for any further intimate interludes with Beatrice.

Chapter 27

A Cash Bonanza

"Your mother must be turning over in her grave," Bea's father declared as he hugged her. "Who would have thought her sister's boy capable of such treachery?"

"I didn't trust him or that fop, Odlum," Glenda muttered, joining the hug.

"There's more, I'm afraid," Bea said. "There's a strong possibility Peter and Odlum killed Malcolm Pickering."

"I knew it all along," Glenda declared. "Said so many a time."

Bea might have laughed had she not been heart-sick about her cousin.

Her father shook his head. "I blame myself for encouraging him. I never considered he might be a murderer."

Bea cradled her beloved father's tear-streaked face. "You trusted him because you always think well of people. It's not a failing."

"Still. To think what might have happened."

"But it didn't, thanks to Roger."

"Yes. His mother was kind enough to collect us from the Grange. We were in a dither how to get here until she arrived."

Bea glanced to where Roger stood nearby with his arm around his mother's waist. She appreciated the concern of both parents and was glad to see them, but the love on Roger's face echoed what she felt. They'd both moved on from the nest. He had become the most important person in her life. They were already one.

Her father walked over to Roger and offered his hand. "Before you ask, you have my undying gratitude as well as my permission to marry my daughter."

Roger beamed as he accepted the gesture, but Lucinda didn't smile. In fact, she stiffened her spine and threw back her shoulders. Bea would have an uphill battle if she hoped to gain Mrs. Sandiford's approval.

Mrs. Barton emerged from the house and invited everyone inside.

They enjoyed several cups of tea while Roger and Bea related the details of the abduction and rescue. Her father and Glenda fleshed out the story with descriptions of their outrage when Bea was abducted.

WHEN BEA laughingly mentioned being trapped in a nest of bank notes scattered around the carriage, Roger realized he'd forgotten that detail. It evidently jolted Mrs. Barton's memory too. "Oh, dear," she exclaimed. "I completely forgot."

She hurried out of the room, returning a few minutes later with a satchel. "We put the money we collected in here," she explained, opening the bag to reveal a cache of bank notes. "As well as the money Mr. Sandiford was able to gather."

"I'm afraid Peter got away with the rest," Roger said. "However, what's left in the bag belongs to you, Baron."

Beatrice's father shook his head. "I'm certain you can find a better use for it than I ever could," he said. "The unemployed need more relief and this windfall can provide it."

A friendly back and forth argument ensued about who should keep the money. It was interrupted by the arrival of Mr. Barton who looked very impressive in his uniform. A hush fell when a heavily whiskered policeman followed him into the drawing room, a dented lockbox tucked under his arm.

Bea stared at the lockbox, recalling the moment it had struck her. Its retrieval could mean many things. Much as she abhorred her cousin's actions, she didn't wish him dead. Her aunt would never understand, and would most likely lay the blame on Bea. There was no guarantee the box contained money. Peter may have ditched it and kept the bank notes when he fled.

"Mr. Leigh is in custody," Barton announced. "He was in a sorry state when my men found him curled up in the shelter of a rock clutching the lockbox. He could scarcely walk and kept muttering something about a black devil."

"Folk claim ghostly beings roam them moors," the policeman said.

"I hate to disappoint you, Constable," Roger said with a smile. "He was probably cursing Midnight, the horse he stole to make his getaway."

"As you say, sir," the policeman replied skeptically.

Mr. Barton took the lockbox and handed it to Bea's father. "I understand this belongs to you, my lord."

After staring at the box for a minute or two, her father passed it to her. "I'll never get used to being a lord. You've a better head on your shoulders than I," he said. "You can decide what to do with it."

"I already know what we're going to use it for," Bea replied. "We'll spend some on the Grange. The rest is for more relief programs for Roger's workers."

For the first time, a trace of a smile tugged at the corners of Lucinda's mouth.

"I'm afraid I'll have to ask you to count the contents of the lockbox and the satchel," Barton said. "For the record when Mr. Leigh is charged with kidnapping and theft at the Assizes. I'll also recommend the Bolton police check with *The Pack Horse* as to when Leigh and Odlum arrived in the town."

"I suspect Odlum never left when he abandoned us at the station," Bea replied. "I have no idea how much should be in the box," she lamented.

"Well," Roger replied. "If the late baron hoarded all the payments I made over the seven years of the mortgage, it should amount to more than £2000."

That possibility brought a broad smile to Lucinda's face.

Roger helped Bea prize the damaged lid open. She gasped when she saw the amount of money the dented box contained. All told, the contents of the box and satchel amounted to £1500. "I've never seen so much money," she exclaimed, eyeing the piles of notes on the Bartons' occasional table.

"Enough to include a fancy wedding in your plans, Miss Parker?" Roger asked, with a teasing glint in his eyes.

"Definitely," she replied.

ROGER DECIDED to ride Midnight back to Bolton, otherwise his spacious brougham would be overcrowded. However, given that the carriage carried two precious burdens—his beloved Beatrice and the large amount of cash—he intended to ride beside the vehicle. Barton provided two constables to ride along with him, so he felt doubly secure.

His decision to ride the horse was based on the hope that Midnight remembered the special bond they'd forged during the frantic ride. It didn't seem so when Gilbert had a devil of a time getting the saddle on the beast, but Midnight calmed when Roger put his foot in the stirrup. "Good lad," he murmured with relief as he swung his leg over and settled in the saddle.

"You look magnificent," Beatrice said, as he trotted into the courtyard. "You belong on that horse."

"I've often thought of selling him," he confessed, feeling smugly magnificent. "He's always been impossible to ride."

"Until now," she said.

"I think he sensed my urgency."

"Well, I'm grateful he did," she replied, turning to follow Lucinda into the brougham.

The Bartons waved and wished them Godspeed as the convoy set off. The journey went smoothly under sunny skies. On the day Beatrice was kidnapped, Roger felt he'd ridden a hundred miles at breakneck speed, yet they reached Bolton at a leisurely pace in a relatively short time.

As long as she lived, Bea would never forget the sight of Roger mounting the temperamental horse. He claimed not to be a good rider, yet he swung his long leg over the beast's back, settled himself in the saddle, and gathered the reins as if he'd ridden for years.

She'd overheard him complain of saddle soreness to the ostler, but could see no sign of discomfort in his posture.

He would be a husband she could depend on and be proud of.

Chapter 28

Planning A Future

Neither Bea nor Roger shared the late baron's distrust of banks. They took the money to the Westminster Bank at the first opportunity. Despite her father's insistence the account be in his daughter's name, the manager refused to honor his wishes. Evidently, the bank's major shareholders believed a woman couldn't be trusted to properly manage such a large amount of money. "Let me guess," she remarked sarcastically to the manager. "Your shareholders are all men."

Her father suggested the account be in her fiancé's name, but Roger protested.

"I see no reason why it shouldn't be in your name," Bea told him. "What difference will it make once we're married?"

So it was agreed, and they subsequently had no trouble making withdrawals when the need arose.

Their first purchase consisted of several hundredweight of coal which they distributed to the homes of Roger's unemployed workers.

New clogs came next, then they hired artisans to teach classes in carpentry, shoemaking, and tailoring. Bea enjoyed shopping for the materials needed for the tailoring classes, but left the purchase of hardware and leather to Roger.

Relieved to have the matter of Pickering's murder solved, Miles Smethurst organized free brass band concerts, and Bea's father offered to give public readings of the Pickwick Papers.

Unemployed workers at other mills soon demanded similar relief programs from their masters. Hampson and his ilk were eventually shamed into loosening their purse strings.

"We make a good team," Bea told Roger on one of the rare occasions when they found themselves alone. "I appreciate your including me in all the decisions."

"I should be thanking you," he replied, gathering her into his embrace. "You're the one with all the good suggestions."

"I was always afraid that, were I to marry, my husband would dismiss my opinions."

"You forget I was raised by Lucinda Sandiford."

Roger meant the comment to be humorous, but mention of his mother saddened Bea. "Do you think your mother will ever accept me?"

BEA'S QUESTION took Roger aback. His fiancée should be busy preparing for her wedding. Instead, she spent most of her time working for the welfare of others. However, she obviously didn't feel comfortable with Lucinda. "She'll come round," he assured her. "She probably won't admit it, but I think she's impressed with your suggestions for relief opportunities. I know she's relieved she can continue to live in Sandiford Manor, and she's aware that's thanks to you and your father."

"That brings up another topic," she said, avoiding his gaze.

"I suspect you're referring to where we'll live after we marry," he replied, having given the matter a lot of thought.

She nodded shyly. "A bride is expected to leave her family and live with her new husband, but I worry about Papa, all alone in that isolated house, except for Glenda."

He had to tread carefully. "I have the same concern about my mother, though our home isn't as isolated as the Grange."

"Nor as dilapidated," she conceded.

"I must admit I've become accustomed to the comforts of Sandiford Manor."

"You'd be too far from the mill out on the moor."

"Half an hour at the most in my brougham. That's not much time and the horses would benefit from the daily drive."

"It would be fun to work on renovating the Grange together."

"I agree," he said, rather surprised he felt comfortable with the prospect.

BEA WAS SECRETLY THRILLED with the prospect of Roger moving into the Grange. She hadn't relished the notion of living in a house ruled by Lucinda Sandiford. She'd already persuaded her father to move out of the master bedroom, and purchased new draperies for the antique four-poster from Whitaker's. She could scarcely wait to share the big bed with Roger and enjoy sensual delights cocooned by the red velvet hangings.

She'd only to remember his clever touch on her most intimate place to become aroused. He'd whispered his intention of tasting her there—*deliciously wicked* didn't begin to describe the intimacies he promised.

Glenda had taken it upon herself to prepare Bea for her wedding night, but her dire warnings bore no relation to the ecstasy she'd already shared with Roger. Of course, she divulged none of that to the maid, who had never been married in any case.

Bea had spent her life in a rural community surrounded by sheep farms, and was no stranger to the mating habits of animals. It had never occurred to her that people carried on in more or less the same fashion, according to Glenda. Men apparently had appendages they inserted into their female partners. Bea found the idea intriguing and not a little scary. The knowledge prompted a secret longing to see Roger's male part for herself.

The provision of a wedding gown was taken out of her hands by, of all people, Lucinda Sandiford. Her future mother-in-law insisted on taking charge of hiring seamstresses and choosing fabric. The fittings took place at Sandiford Manor, and Lucinda was present at every session, offering opinions which Bea sensibly agreed with. She deemed it preferable not to mention the possibility Roger might move out to the Grange. Let him inform his unpredictable mother.

ROGER HAD NEVER BEEN RULED by his baser instincts. Now, he was in a constant state of arousal whenever he was with Beatrice. Even if they were apart, thinking of her had his cock at full salute. Wicked thoughts ran riot in his imagination when he learned she'd charged red velvet bed hangings to his account at Whitaker's.

Beatrice's apparent desire to create an enticingly sensual bedroom confirmed his belief a passionate woman lurked beneath her conservative demeanor. Her response to his intimate touching proved it. At first, he'd been hesitant to whisper of future sexual delights, but she seemed as anxious as he to experience the joys to be found in the marriage bed.

He considered himself a lucky man. Hampson and many of the other mill masters boasted openly of their mistresses. Roger had a feeling Beatrice would more than satisfy his husbandly needs.

Chapter 29

Scandalous Proposal

What with the bridal fittings and the classes for the workers, Beatrice spent quite a lot of time during the day at Sandiford Manor. Roger invited both her and her father to stay for dinner one evening to discuss improvements to the mill. The ventilation systems he had in mind would be costly, and he didn't feel he had the right to make the decision himself.

During the dinner, Lucinda proved to be a surprisingly jovial hostess, laughing at all Arthur's attempts to inject witty remarks into the conversation. She was still a beautiful woman—when she smiled.

After they'd enjoyed the sweet course, Roger embarked on his plan. "I'd prefer we not adjourn for cigars," he said to Arthur. "I'd like to discuss installing a ventilation system for the mill."

"I'd rather hoped Beatrice and I could have a little *tête-à-tête* in your absence," Lucinda replied.

"We can chat afterwards, if you like," Beatrice suggested.

Roger was relieved by how easily his mother acquiesced.

"What are you proposing?" Arthur asked.

"The best quote I have is from Dobson and Barlow on Kay Street. They can start the work almost immediately."

"I should think they'd be glad of the contract, given the situation with the cotton famine," Lucinda said.

"But they do have a good reputation, from what I've heard," Arthur said. "How much is the quote?"

"£100, which includes the carding and spinning rooms, but not the weaving room."

It was a princely sum, so Arthur's hesitation didn't surprise him.

"I can't think of anything more important on which to spend £100," Beatrice said. "It's a lifesaving measure and we can well afford it."

"I agree," Lucinda and Arthur chimed in together, which led to an exchange of curious smiles between the two. Roger couldn't recall ever seeing his mother blush before.

"Now that's settled," Lucinda said. "Why don't you gentlemen run along and leave us ladies to our little chat?"

The apprehension on Beatrice's face caused Roger to hesitate, but he could hardly argue when Arthur rose from the table. "We'll adjourn to my study," he told his future father-in-law. "I've a French brandy I'm confident you'll enjoy."

"Let's adjourn to the drawing room, shall we?" Lucinda suggested, in an unfriendly tone that only increased Bea's nervousness.

"Certainly," she replied.

"I'll get straight to the point," her future mother-in-law said as soon as they were seated.

Bea might have made some remark about that not being out of character, but she thought better of it.

"You should rethink your decision to have Roger move into Belmont Grange."

This too shouldn't have been a surprise, but the suggestion raised Bea's hackles. "It wasn't *my* decision," she retorted. "We talked it over and both agreed."

Lucinda stuck out her chin. "Roger would agree to anything he thought pleased you."

Bea seethed. Roger had apparently had second thoughts and spoken to his mother about the matter. "Are you saying he doesn't want to move to Belmont Grange?"

"No, it's my opinion that Belmont Grange is your father's baronial seat. He should remain master there. A house cannot have two masters, and my son is used to ruling his own household."

Bea hated to admit it, but Lucinda was right, except for the fact it was common knowledge *she* ruled Sandiford House, not Roger. Her father hadn't objected to giving up his bedroom, but it wasn't in his nature to be confrontational. However, the alternative was for Bea to move into Sandiford House, an option that held no appeal. "A house cannot have two mistresses, either," she said, well aware she risked Lucinda's anger.

"I agree, and I have no wish to live under your rule here," Lucinda replied, with more than a hint of condescension. "I have therefore suggested to your father that I move to Belmont Grange as his housekeeper."

Bea couldn't breathe. Lucinda and her father? Living together in the same house? "And what did he say to that proposal?" she asked, dreading the answer.

"He suggested it."

WHEN HE AND Arthur joined the ladies in the drawing room after a pleasant, brandy-fueled discussion about American politics, Roger sensed the tension. However, his future father-in-law spoke while Roger was dithering about how best to broach whatever it was the women had argued over.

"I see you've told my daughter about our proposition," Arthur said to Lucinda.

"She has," Beatrice replied testily. "It's inappropriate and out of the question."

"My presence at Belmont Grange would be no more inappropriate than Glenda's," Lucinda retorted.

Roger shook his head. "Will somebody tell me what's going on?"

"Your mother thinks you and I should live here after we are married, and she will move into the Grange with my father."

"As my housekeeper," Arthur insisted.

Roger understood Beatrice's anger. She saw Lucinda's plan as an underhanded plot to replace her late mother. "Well," he said, selfishly worried about missing out on making love to Beatrice cocooned by red velvet hangings. "It's an interesting proposal."

"Interesting?" Beatrice exclaimed. "It's scandalous!"

Roger suddenly knew how the Allied infantry at Waterloo felt when the French cavalry attacked. "Would you like to be mistress of Sandiford Manor?" he asked, hoping to break down her resistance bit by bit.

"Well ... er ... yes," Beatrice admitted. "It's a fine house. But ..."

"But you wouldn't be mistress if my mother continued to live here."

"No," she agreed weakly, blushing profusely.

"Lucinda is thinking of you," Arthur said. "Don't you see that?"

"But she can't take Mama's place," Beatrice wailed.

"No one could ever do that," her father agreed. "Nor would Lucinda wish to do so."

"We're not suggesting anything improper," Lucinda insisted, her nose in the air. "We're simply trying to make everyone happy."

A long silence ensued. Roger was tempted to suggest he and Beatrice purchase a new fourposter to replace the bed in his chamber at Sandiford Manor, but decided this perhaps wasn't the right moment.

"I suppose we could consider the plan," Beatrice allowed.

Relieved, and not caring if he offended either parent, he took her into his embrace. "I think it's the best option," he whispered close to her ear.

Chapter 30

Renovations

In the two weeks leading up to the wedding, Belmont Grange became the scene of frenzied activity that had nothing to do with the blessed event. Having inspected her proposed new residence, Lucinda decreed the kitchen was to be modernized. Bea kept to herself the opinion that Lucinda was unlikely to do any cooking. Glenda, of course, was all in favor of many of the proposed improvements.

A cast-iron range was purchased and installed, replacing the ancient wood-stove. It consisted of two ovens with a cast-iron plate on top, and a sealed chimney. It was identical to the one in Sandiford Manor. Lucinda declared it smoke free and fuel efficient.

"This kitchen was built as far from the living rooms as possible, which is a good thing," Lucinda opined with satisfaction. "So, no smoke, smells, or noises can penetrate the living areas and fire hazards are kept far away."

Each time she visited, she came with a copy of *Mrs. Beeton's Book of Household Management,* and shared much of its contents with the workmen hired to bring the kitchen up to scratch.

"At least this kitchen is on the cooler side of the house and it does face north, though we may have to move the door in order to avoid draughts near the fireplace. Fortunately, we have high ceilings which will help to keep the room cool. We might have to install high windows to allow hot air to escape. That will keep lower wall space free for cupboards and shelves."

The laborers gaped as if she'd spoken in Greek.

"Let's not get too carried away, Mama," Roger advised, echoing Bea's sentiments.

"The range will need a lot of coal," Lucinda carried on as if Roger had said nothing. "So it's to the good that the coal store and scullery are right next to the kitchen. We'll also require a wine cellar, a dry goods store, a vegetable store, a game larder including hanging racks, a fish larder, all separate and specifically designed to house their contents."

Roger and Bea exchanged exasperated glances.

Mrs. Beeton's opus contained over 900 recipes. After a quick perusal, Glenda declared many of them were designed for the rich, to which Lucinda replied that while the diet of poorer folk may consist of bread, butter, potatoes, beer, and tea, Baron Belmont deserved far better.

Bea couldn't argue with her logic. Studies had proven that the poor often suffered from anemia and rickets, thanks to their impoverished diet.

"We'll serve the main meal of the day in the early evening," Lucinda announced. "It will consist of soup, roasted meat with potatoes, two vegetable side dishes, rolls with butter, jams, jellies and sweet pickles, cake and preserved fruit, coffee, hot punch, and water."

"Crikey!" Glenda exclaimed. "I'm expected to cook all that?"

"No. I intend to hire a real cook, and of course, we'll need the proper cutlery for each course."

Nose out of joint at the notion she wasn't *a real cook,* Glenda muttered, "More washing up."

Lucinda insisted Bea accompany her on several trips to Manchester to purchase items which would be impossible to find in Bolton. They returned with rotating spice racks, steampowered spits, jelly molds, and can openers.

This flurry of activity had nothing directly to do with her wedding, yet Bea found herself caught up in Lucinda's enthusiasm. She even purchased her own copy of Mrs. Beeton's book and a few new copper pans Lucinda insisted the cook at Sandiford Manor would appreciate.

Remarkably, by the time the eve of the wedding arrived, in addition to the cast-iron range, the old kitchen sported a new tile floor, a brass tap that provided cold running water, a huge rectangular table, and a dresser which held cooking equipment, utensils, and some crockery. The walls had been freshly whitewashed and decorated with the motto, *Waste Not, Want Not.* Glenda was particularly impressed that running water meant an end to going out to the pump in the yard in all weathers.

KNOWING Beatrice was due to teach a mathematics class, an impatient Roger waited for her in his study. In some ways, it was a good thing the mill was idle, because he spent most of his time with his fiancée. He craved the sound of her voice, the taste of her lips, the touch of her hands on his face, the weight of her breast in his hand. "I'm sorry my mother's plans have caused so much upheaval at the Grange," he told her when she appeared. The students hadn't yet arrived so he put his arms around her waist and gathered her close. Inevitably, his male body became aroused.

"Actually," she replied. "The improvements were sorely

needed, and the project has given us the chance to get to know one another better."

"Mama hasn't mentioned it but I know she enjoyed having you accompany her to Manchester."

"Did Philippa never go to the city with her?"

"Yes, but you know what my sister's like. Shopping expeditions were all about what *she* wanted."

"And your mother paid for it."

"Exactly, or I did in the long run."

She put her hands on his shoulders. "My students will be here soon," she said, worrying her bottom lip.

"I don't care. My workers know we are to marry on the morrow. They won't be scandalized if they find us embracing. I'm not sure why you're even here. Nobody expects you to be working today."

She averted her gaze. "I know. I confess I'm glad to get away from Lucinda and her kitchen for a while. Sorry."

"Don't apologize. I find her too much sometimes."

"It's generous of her to move to the Grange."

"Oh, I'm sure her motives aren't altogether selfless." He regretted the insinuation as soon as the words were uttered.

"What do you mean by that?" she asked, pulling away.

He refused to let her go, despite her efforts to be free. Naturally, two of his young workers chose that unfortunate moment to enter the study.

Chapter 31

Holy Trinity

O n the eve of the wedding, Lucinda insisted Bea stay overnight in Philippa's old room at Sandiford Manor. In her opinion, it was out of the question for a bride to travel all the way to Holy Trinity from the moor. Bea agreed, provided Glenda was allowed to accompany her. She sensed the maid would be terribly hurt if denied the opportunity to help prepare Bea for her wedding.

Lucinda decreed Roger and Bea not see each other that evening, but Roger sent a message that he was waiting in his study and wanted to kiss her goodnight.

He rose from his chair by the hearth when she entered. They clung together for long minutes. She tensed, sensing he had something on his mind.

"Come, sit by the fire," he said, taking her hand. "I have a confession to make."

Her legs suddenly felt like jelly, but she managed to walk to the chair. He stood in front of the fireplace, legs braced.

"You're making me nervous," she admitted.

"It's not my intention, but there are things you should know about me before we marry."

A thousand replies came to mind, but she deemed it preferable to remain silent and listen.

"I grew up in the slums of Bolton," he said. "In a cellar dwelling like the Mann family."

The news took her aback, but a dreadful start in life only made his success that much more impressive. "All the more justification for my admiration of what you've achieved."

"That's not all. I didn't know my father. It's likely I'm a bastard, though only Lucinda knows for sure. It has taken years of ruthless wheeling and dealing to get where I am. I will never be a gentleman."

To her shame, Bea realized the toll her snobbishness had taken on him. He thought he wasn't worthy of her. She rose and took his warm hands. "You have behaved in a gentlemanly manner since the first day I met you. I, on the other hand, judged you harshly because you were a tradesman, but I've learned a person's worth has nothing to do with birth or rank. I am the one who must strive hard to be your equal."

Shaking his head, he swallowed hard and put his arms around her. "I love you, Beatrice," he sighed.

"As I love you, Roger."

"Until tomorrow, my beautiful bride."

They shared a loving kiss before she took her leave.

BEA WAS PLEASED WHEN, shortly after dawn, her maid was part of the giddy contingent that brought her breakfast in bed. The other maids seemed happy to have Glenda as part of their teasing group.

Having enjoyed her lightly boiled eggs and toast, she had to admit that being pampered in the boudoir was a great pleasure. Moving to Sandiford Manor had its advantages. She suspected

he recognized many of his workers. He sensed their reluctance to enter. Most Lancashire working-class folk weren't adherents of the Anglican faith, so he encouraged them to follow him into the church. "I'll wager most will choose to sit on the bride's side of the aisle," he told Miles.

"Aye, think the world of Miss Parker, they do," his best man agreed.

The pews seemed disappointingly empty, but Miles was right that they'd arrived early.

They went first to the vestry to assure the vicar all was proceeding as planned, then took their seats in the front pew.

"I suppose I should be nervous," Roger confided. "Strangely, I'm not."

"It's a sign tha's weddin' the right woman, Master," Miles replied. "And I'm honored to be tha best man."

"There was a time I was jealous of you," Roger confessed. "I thought you had feelings for Miss Parker."

"Me?" Miles exclaimed, swiveling his head. "Nay. Anybody could see reet off she were meant fer thee."

As the first subdued notes of organ music drifted to his ears, Roger pondered his overseer's words. As soon as he set eyes on Beatrice Parker at Great Moor Street station, not too far from this very church, his heart and his body had told him she was the one. Preoccupied with business woes and the murder investigation, he just hadn't listened well enough.

WHEN SHE EMERGED from Sandiford Manor, Bea was greeted by rousing cheers from people she recognized as Roger's workers, among them Bridget's sister and father, as well as several of her young students. She'd come to respect these hard-working men and women. Often enduring intolerable living conditions, they were the life blood of Lancashire's prosperity, and she was humbled by their affection for her.

After she was settled in the brougham, Glenda and her father assisted with stuffing the long train of her gown into the carriage. She'd have preferred a much simpler style, but Lucinda had insisted on the ostentatious design. Cocooned in yards of satin, Bea, her father, and Glenda set off for the church. Bea was pleased her lifelong maid was accompanying her to the most important event of her life. In many ways, Glenda had been more of a mother to her than Abigail Parker.

At Holy Trinity, getting her out of the carriage proved to be even more of a challenge for her companions. She'd wanted to appoint Glenda as her maid of honor, but Lucinda protested that choosing a servant was out of the question and Philippa was the obvious choice. Gowned in a bejeweled frock more suitable for a ball, Philippa stood in the doorway of the church, sporting her usual pout. She remained rooted to the spot, clearly having no intention of assisting her future sister-in-law. Frustrated, Bea's spirits lifted when Meg Mann appeared to help Glenda. They kept Bea's train from trailing on the mucky pathway. Tempted to ask them to carry the train all the way up the aisle, Bea nevertheless refrained. Philippa might cry off in a fit of pique and she'd never hear the end of it from Lucinda. This was Roger's day as well as hers, so for his sake, she wouldn't cause an uproar. But the experience confirmed what she'd learned during her time in Lancashire. Class and wealth didn't determine a person's worth.

Chapter 32

Matrimony

W aiting for his bride, Roger sensed people filing into the pews behind him. Miles had no hesitation in turning round to check. "Fillin' up," he declared with satisfaction.

Roger felt proud when he heard his mother's name being whispered. No doubt she was marching up the aisle, head held high. He loved and respected Lucinda Sandiford and owed much of his success to her sacrifices, but peace filled his heart when he acknowledged that a different woman now held dominion over him. Beatrice had come into his life and changed the future completely. They shared love of a different sort. Duty would bind them, but passion had already united their souls.

He looked back at his mother as she took her rightful place of honor in the pew behind him. She didn't return his smile, but sparkling eyes told him she was happy for him.

Suddenly realizing he'd been holding his breath, he rose with the rest of the congregation when the organ announced his bride's arrival.

When he turned, it vaguely registered that the church was packed. Every eye followed the smiling bride. He too couldn't take his eyes off the beautiful woman walking toward him. The white gown's neckline was modest yet it revealed enough of her tantalizing bounty to harden his arousal. Her burnished hair was piled into an elaborate arrangement, her neck caressed by curling tendrils designed to drive a man mad. He couldn't wait to pull the red glory loose. Her laughing eyes suggested she knew what he was thinking.

He barely noticed his sister trailing far behind an enormously long train until she came level with Beatrice and took her bouquet of yellow roses. Stunned when Philippa bestowed a genuine smile on him, he was jolted back to the solemn reality of the proceedings when Arthur placed Beatrice's delicate hand in his.

"I love you," he whispered—three little words that didn't begin to describe the emotion filling his heart.

"DEARLY BELOVED, we are gathered here in the sight of God and in the face of this congregation, to join together this man and this woman in holy matrimony."

The vicar's introduction was an abrupt reminder for Bea that they were in a holy place, and throwing herself into the arms of the smiling man she loved would be deemed inappropriate. She struggled to control her rapidly beating heart and bowed her head. Roger's thumb tracing circles in her palm didn't lessen the heat flooding her body. The naughty man knew very well he was making matters worse.

She held her breath when the vicar asked if anyone knew of any impediment to their marriage. She half expected Peter to shout his objections, a scenario she admitted inwardly was nonsensical because he was in prison.

She chastised herself when it became evident the vicar had finished his preamble and moved on to the vows.

"Roger Sandiford, wilt thou have this woman to thy wedded wife, to live together according to God's law in the holy estate of matrimony? Wilt thou love her, comfort her, honor and keep her, in sickness and in health; and, forsaking all other, keep thee only unto her, so long as ye both shall live?"

"I will," he replied, squeezing her hand.

"Beatrice Abigail Parker, wilt thou have this man to thy wedded husband, to live together after God's ordinance in the holy estate of matrimony? Wilt thou obey him, and serve him, love, honor, and keep him, in sickness and in health; and, forsaking all other, keep thee only unto him, so long as ye both shall live?"

She looked into Roger's loving gaze as she vowed, "I will."

Following the vicar's prompts, they each promised to be faithful to each other for better, for worse, for richer, for poorer, in sickness and in health, to love and to cherish, till death parted them.

Miles stepped forward and placed a ring on the Bible. The vicar blessed it before offering it to Roger. Her bridegroom took hold of her trembling hand and slipped the ring on her finger. "With this ring I thee wed," he said. "With my body I thee honor, and all my worldly goods with thee I share. In the name of the Father, and of the Son, and of the Holy Ghost. Amen."

Bea was reminded of a time when she'd been tempted to settle her hand in his. Her heart had known then that Roger was her soulmate. She relished the warm strength of his hand as she murmured, "I love you."

The vicar then bade them kneel and invoked a prayer. "O eternal God, Creator and Preserver of all mankind, giver of all spiritual grace, the author of everlasting life, send thy blessing upon these thy servants, this man and this woman, whom we bless in thy name; that, living faithfully together, they may surely perform and keep the vow and covenant betwixt them made, whereof this ring given and received is a token and pledge; and may ever remain in perfect love and peace together, and live according to thy laws. Through Jesus Christ our Lord."

"Amen," resounded from the congregation.

Perfect love and peace sounded like heaven to Bea.

"Those whom God hath joined together let no man put asunder," the vicar announced. "Forasmuch as Roger and Beatrice have consented together in holy wedlock, and have witnessed the same before God and this company, and thereto have given and pledged their troth either to other, and have declared the same by giving and receiving of a ring, and by joining of hands, I pronounce that they be man and wife together, in the name of the Father, and of the Son, and of the Holy Ghost. Amen."

Rising from her knees, Bea pursed her lips, expecting Roger to be given permission to kiss her, but the vicar then commenced the order of service for communion.

By the time the epistle, the gospel, the eucharist, and the final prayers were offered, she was desperate to lose herself in Roger's embrace. When the vicar gave leave for a kiss, the congregation cheered as their lips met. They were still clapping and whistling a full five minutes later. The vicar's polite cough broke them apart.

Chapter 33

Buffet

When Bea leaned forward to sign her name to the register in the vestry, Roger twirled his finger into one of the tendrils of her hair. "I've been itching to do this since I saw you walking down the aisle," he whispered, lest the vicar overhear.

She smiled coyly, her mind obviously on the same things as his. He put his arm round her waist while Philippa signed as a witness. He was surprised when Miles made his mark instead of signing his name. It had never occurred to him his overseer was illiterate. In fact, he was certain Smethurst could read his orders. It seemed his literacy competency didn't extend to signing his own name on an important document. Clearly, there was much work to be done in terms of education.

But that was for the future. He offered his arm to his blushing bride and escorted her back into the church. Her father hugged her and shook Roger's hand. Lucinda kissed Beatrice on each cheek and hugged Roger, who then escorted his bride down the aisle and out of the church. The long train of her gown made for slow going. Outside, they were pelted with rice on their way to the carriage. Sweating when he finally managed to stuff the voluminous train into the carriage, he climbed aboard and joined his giggling wife. "Don't blame me," she said between hiccups. "The train was your mother's idea."

"I just hope it's easier to remove entirely," he replied, grateful for her steadying hand when the carriage lurched forward.

In their cozy nest of white satin, they indulged in toe-curling kisses and intimate touching. "Let's forego the reception my mother has arranged and go straight to my bedroom," he said.

"I'd love nothing better," she replied, "but Lucinda would come and drag us out of bed."

"True," he conceded, grinning like a youth in the first flush of sexual awareness. "Let's hope the speeches are short."

UPON THEIR ARRIVAL at Sandiford Manor, Roger was ushered into the dining room. Meanwhile, maids whisked Bea upstairs into a guest bedroom where the seamstresses deftly unpicked the stitches that attached the long train to the gown. She resented spending even one minute apart from her new husband, but it was a relief to be free of the weight and sit down for a brief respite. A maid thrust a glass of champagne into her hands. She closed her eyes and took a gulp, instantly regretting the impulse when bubbles stole up her nose and made her cough. "I'm not used to spirits," she told the worried maid, preferring not to mention she'd never drunk alcohol in her life.

A breathless Glenda arrived and fussed with her hair. "Leave a few tendrils loose," she told her maid, who simply nodded knowingly.

"Guests have started to arrive," Lucinda announced when she entered the room. "We must organize the receiving line."

Several minutes later, guests began to file through the line, showering congratulations on the happy couple, the parents, and Roger's sister and her husband. "I'm astonished to see your brother-in-law does actually know how to smile," she whispered to Roger during a brief lull.

He meshed his fingers with hers and raised her hand to his lips. It was a thrilling gesture that was becoming familiar. "I don't see Philippa enduring Josiah for much longer," he replied, bending his head to whisper in her ear.

Bea pitied Philippa then, trapped in a loveless marriage. "We're so lucky," she said.

He merely nodded when another guest claimed his attention, but she knew he understood.

The formalities taken care of, the newlyweds took their places at the head table and the guests heeded Lucinda's invitation to be seated.

~

Lucinda Sandiford's lavish dinner parties were famous among Bolton's well-to-do. Also aware of her reputation for impatience, the hundred or so guests were quickly seated, every expectant face turned toward Roger's mother, who stood with arms folded at the front of the room.

The mayor of Bolton, town councilors, mill owners, dignitaries from the local constabulary, judges, barristers, bank managers—they and their wives all waited politely for Lucinda to begin the festivities.

Even the servants carrying platters from the kitchen to the groaning board were careful not to make a sound.

"I'm pleased to see the Barton brothers in attendance with their spouses," Roger whispered to Beatrice, earning a reproving glare from his mother.

His wife's naughty grin didn't temper his urge to burst out laughing.

"Welcome one and all," Lucinda began when complete silence reigned. "I'd ask the Reverend to say Grace, after which the head table will proceed to the buffet. The word *buffet* comes from the French for the side table where feasts were set out in medieval times. Guests will be informed by a footman when it is their table's turn to partake."

The vicar who had married them dutifully led the gathering in Grace. His mother then took her place at the head table and nodded to Roger. "Does your father know what he's in for?' he asked Beatrice, as he led her by the hand to the buffet table.

"He probably does now," she replied.

BEA ACKNOWLEDGED it was a forlorn hope, but she wished more than one of her husband's employees had been invited. Only Miles Smethurst was there, and Roger had confided his mother wasn't too pleased with his choice of the overseer as his best man. Even Glenda had been forbidden to attend the banquet.

"Meg's eyes would pop out of her head if she saw all this food," she said to Roger.

"I told my mother to spare no expense," he confessed, as he heaped slices of roast beef on both their plates. "I see she took me at my word."

"I think we'd be having a much rowdier celebration if you'd invited some of the workers."

"True," he agreed. "We can arrange something less formal with them in a day or two."

It gladdened her heart that he understood how she felt. "I don't feel at home with this crowd."

"Neither do I," he confessed. "However, it's expected, and if anyone can impress Bolton's well-to-do, it's my mother."

~

Anxious to take Beatrice to bed, Roger prayed the speeches would be mercifully short. Like many Lancashire mill workers, Miles was a man of few words. However, the mayor had been known to waffle on, mainly extolling his own contributions to the town's wellbeing. Roger had gritted his teeth when informed by his mother that Roderick Hampson had requested an opportunity to say a few words.

In the event, it was Miles who rambled on about Roger's success as Master of Broadclough Mill, and how his compassion and good works had earned the esteem of his workers. Roger noted Hampson's face getting redder and redder. He was one of the few who didn't raise his glass when Miles finally proposed a toast to the newlyweds.

The mayor spoke briefly about *the ridiculous American Civil War* that had transformed Lancashire cotton workers from the most prosperous in the country to the most impoverished. He touted his own efforts to spearhead public works projects such as cleaning rivers, landscaping parks, and surfacing roads which would employ destitute cotton workers.

To Roger's amazement, Hampson acknowledged Roger's relief projects had inspired many of his fellow mill owners.

Arthur Parker was called upon to toast the bride. His voice filled with love and pride, he told the guests how proud Beatrice's mother would be of her daughter.

Tears trickled down Beatrice's cheeks as the guests drank to her health and happiness.

Roger was taken aback when his mother rose from her seat and raised her glass. He steeled himself for caustic remarks, probably at his expense, but Lucinda surprised him. "Now," she announced. "I'm certain you'll all understand if my son whisks his bride off to bed."

Roger grinned as he lifted a blushing Beatrice and carried her out of the dining room to loud applause.

Chapter 34

Fulfillment

Bea had never been an outgoing person. She had only one lifelong female friend and no experience relating to men. Roger was the exception. She felt comfortable with him. However, they were about to embark on an aspect of married life of which she had no knowledge, except for the brief interludes of intimate touching she and Roger had indulged in.

She'd giggled and become excited when he'd teased about sexual delights to come. Today, she'd sensed a growing tension in him that suggested more than simple delight was involved in their joining.

"I'm nervous," she confessed, as her husband kicked open the door of his chamber and carried her over the threshold.

"That's natural," he replied, setting her on her feet. "I'd be worried if you weren't nervous."

Fearing her knees might buckle, she was glad he kept his arms around her waist.

"Do you know what's going to happen between us?" he asked.

Looking into brown eyes full of love, Bea realized she was

woefully ignorant. "Glenda warned me there'll be pain when you ... er ...."

She didn't expect his teasing laughter. "Poor Glenda," he quipped. "There might be pain when I penetrate your maidenhead, but I promise you it will be fleeting. Trust me. Our joining will be magical, my darling Beatrice."

"I do trust you," she replied honestly. It would be an honor to surrender her prized virginity to this man she loved. "I want to be yours."

~

ROGER'S HEART and loins rejoiced. "I never expected to find a love like ours," he confessed. "You honor me with your love."

Her lips were too close to resist. She opened readily for him when their mouths met. His insistent cock mimicked his tongue as it thrust in and out of her sweet mouth. Her tongue teased his, her hips matching the rhythm set by his. He tasted the sherry trifle served for dessert and a faint hint of champagne. Mostly, she tasted of pure woman.

His hands found their way into her hair. It was an easy matter to pull out the pins. His arousal hardened when the red glory cascaded over her shoulders and caressed his hands. Detecting the tantalizing aroma of female arousal, he groaned, itching to see his bride naked.

"I'm afraid there are lots of buttons," she murmured into his mouth when his hands wandered to the back of the gown.

"Maybe you should turn round," he replied, barely holding on to his control when she complied and lifted the burnished tresses off her nape.

Lots of buttons turned out to be at least a million of the infernal fasteners that kept him from his goal. Taking a deep breath, he forced his trembling hands to undo each one in turn.

Like most men, he'd always been drawn to women's breasts, but as the length of Beatrice's spine was revealed, he had a new appreciation for the perfect beauty of a woman's back. He bestowed kisses as he went, smugly pleased when she shivered. His demure Beatrice was fast becoming as impatient for the joining as he was.

When he reached her waist, he delved his hands inside the bodice and cupped her breasts, beyond relieved she wasn't wearing a corset. The gown fell away as she arched her back, mewling when he brushed a thumb over each nipple.

She leaned forward to ease the gown off over her hips. The press of her bottom against his rampant manhood was sweet torture. Impatient to see her naked, he took over pushing the gown and the petticoats off her body. "I remember these," he exclaimed when only her pantalets remained.

Preoccupied with her unmentionables since the carriage wreck, he abruptly decided this was the perfect moment to fulfill his fantasy.

Delaying his desire to see her completely bare, he scooped her up, carried her to the bed, and knelt between her legs. "Yes," he growled, upon discovering no fabric between him and the glistening pink folds. Heart beating wildly and cock nigh on ready to burst, he curled his arms around her thighs, lowered his mouth to her most intimate place, and feasted on her juices.

It occurred to Bea she hadn't fully understood Roger's teasing promises. Putting his mouth on her most private part wasn't just a passing fancy for him. He was clearly under some sort of spell. Nor had she realized the effect his tongue's attentions would have on her.

There was more to this intimate joining than she'd thought.

It was as if Roger's male instincts were controlling him now, and she liked this dominant side of him.

She tried to analyze the new feelings blossoming deep within her own body, but soon gave up. This rapture was to be savored. She sifted her fingers through his silky hair, idly wondering if sexual congress involved him eventually taking off his clothes too.

The notion to ask him fled when a crescendo of desire began in her womb and flooded every fibre of her being. She closed her eyes as wave after wave of ecstasy carried her into a world of rainbows. She shouted her euphoria when the throbbing void inside her was filled. Her shout of joy quickly turned to a scream when pain arrowed through her.

"I'm sorry, my love," Roger rasped. "I couldn't wait. The pain will pass."

She opened her eyes. Roger lay atop her, his manhood pulsing inside her.

Roger cursed his lack of finesse. He had planned to gradually introduce his virgin bride to the notion of penetration. Instead, he'd barely had time to undo the falls of his trousers before thrusting inside her, and if he didn't move soon, he might go mad.

"You're still dressed," she murmured, disappointment evident in her green eyes. "I wanted to see you naked."

His greedy cock insisted he remind her they would be married for many years and eventually ...

Gritting his teeth, he knew he had to comport himself more like a gentleman. He slid from her body, felt foolish hopping about on one foot to remove his shoes, and finally managed to tear off his clothes. Breathing hard and ready to burst, he stood naked beside the bed.

When she stared at his rampant cock, he tried to think of calm, reassuring words. He could tell her God had been generous but his size wouldn't matter. He clamped his mouth shut when it dawned on him that what shimmered in the green depths was hungry desire, not fear.

He groaned when she reached out and touched a finger to his swollen tip. "Are you going to put it back?" she asked coyly.

His heart bursting, he climbed onto the bed, positioned himself at her opening, looked into her eyes and thrust.

"No pain this time," she whispered, moving her hips provocatively.

"Good," he replied, matching her rhythm.

It didn't take long for them to reach their climax together.

Dizzied by euphoric joy, he called out his beloved's name as his seed erupted from his body and she screamed her fulfillment.

Chapter 35

Wedded Bliss

L ucinda moved to Belmont Grange the day after the wedding. She absolutely refused to take any of her furniture, insisting Roger and his new wife would need it. As it was, transporting her clothing and what she referred to as *personal knick-knacks* took most of the day. Bea was astonished at the extent of her mother-in-law's varied wardrobe, since she'd only ever seen Lucinda in the same high-necked, black bombazine frock. It was intriguing to wonder when and where Lucinda had worn the stylish clothing, but she didn't yet know her well enough to ask.

It took less than a week for the relationship between Lucinda and Glenda to break down completely. To no one's surprise, it turned out they couldn't tolerate each other. Glenda claimed the cook hired by Lucinda treated her like a scullery maid. Bea was happy to have Glenda come to Sandiford Manor as her personal maid. She herself spent much of her time teaching; familiarizing herself with her new responsibilities as mistress of Sandiford Manor sometimes felt a little overwhelming. She was glad the servants seemed to like her, but it was important they respect her as well. It would be too easy for them to think they could get away with things Lucinda would never have tolerated.

Roger worked with the men from Dobson and Barlow's to settle on the details for the mill's proposed ventilation system. He took care of the delivery of relief supplies to his unemployed workers. The newlyweds didn't always wait until after the evening meal to fall into bed together, both hungry for the sexual delights they shared.

Nor did they always make it as far as their bed. Bea wasn't shocked to discover her insatiable husband had all kinds of creative ideas about places to indulge in sexual congress. The desk in his office proved to be one of his favorites. The memory of the delights they'd shared caused her to blush profusely during the mathematics lessons she conducted in his study during the day. She hoped the young students had no reason to suspect what went on there in the evenings.

When they bathed together, Bea was proud to wash her husband's magnificent body. The wooden bathtub wasn't big enough for two, so they took turns to cleanse each other after making love.

Brought up by God-fearing parents, Bea had always considered herself a genteel young lady. Who would have thought she'd turn out to be a wanton who craved her husband's mouth on her most intimate place? Or that she'd enjoy feasting on that marvelous piece of male equipment her husband called his *cock*.

They were happy, but looming over their married bliss was Peter's upcoming trial. Bea supposed it was understandable in the circumstances that her aunt and uncle hadn't attended her wedding, but their absence was worrisome. She hadn't written to them, having no idea what she would say. Nor had she had any word from them.

Halliwell had been assigned to another case involving a murder at the local music hall. All he could tell the Sandifords was that the trial would be conducted at the Manchester Assizes. Bea dreaded it, but the ordeal had to be faced.

ROGER TRIED hard to concentrate on business matters, but his thoughts continually drifted to his beautiful wife. Since his home was right next door to the mill, it was too easy to leave work and coax Beatrice into removing her clothes. Not that she needed much coaxing. He sometimes wondered if the constant drive to enjoy each other's bodies would fade with time. He hoped not.

Each was learning how and where the other liked to be touched. They were also learning to share a home together and he was confident they were happy in their new life, especially with his mother out on the moor. Beatrice had stepped easily into the role of mistress of Sandiford Manor. The servants clearly loved her. He felt reborn—like a youth who's just discovered the joys of sexual release and can't get enough of it.

There was just one fly in the ointment. Beatrice never spoke of her cousin and his crimes, but he sensed she was dreading the upcoming trial.

He too wanted to be free of the memories of the dark times when a murderer roamed free and he'd feared for his darling Beatrice.

They'd been married three weeks when notification came. They would both be required to testify at Peter Leigh's trial scheduled for a month hence.

EARLY IN THE morning on the day of the trial, Bea, Roger, and both parents traveled to Manchester in the brougham. Glenda stayed in Bolton after being informed servants weren't allowed to testify against a member of the gentry. "I don't fault her outrage," Bea told Roger. "Peter might not belong to one of the lower classes but he killed a boy, stole money, and kidnapped me. Glenda is a much better person."

She tried to relax and enjoy the ride. She'd never imagined she would be married to a man who owned such a splendid vehicle pulled by two magnificent horses, but today, the splendor meant nothing.

Winged creatures fluttered in her belly. The prospect of relating her shameful ordeal in front of complete strangers couldn't be borne.

The accused was her cousin—a fact that reflected badly on her whole family. If her mother hadn't already succumbed to illness, these tragic circumstances would have polished her off.

The rural scenery en route was pleasant, until they reached the city proper where industry reigned. In Philippa's estimation, Manchester was almost on a par with London. Bea had never been to London, and had no wish to visit a big city if Manchester was a prime example.

Her previous visits with Lucinda had involved shopping. No such frivolity lay in store on this occasion.

"Dirty place," Lucinda muttered.

Bea might have chuckled. Lucinda lived in Bolton—not the cleanest of towns.

All too soon, they arrived at the Assizes. Roger held her hand tightly as they proceeded into the courthouse.

Chapter 36

Trial

U pon arrival at the courthouse in Manchester, Lucinda hurried away to secure a seat in the gallery. Roger, Bea, and her father were led to an anteroom reserved for witnesses where they were instructed to wait. She recognized most of the people waiting in the anteroom with them. Thaddeus Barton was there, as was Sergeant Halliwell. Roger identified the man she didn't know as the manager of the Westminster Bank where he dealt.

The one complete stranger eventually approached Bea's father. "I assume you are Baron Belmont," he said, extending a hand. "Allow me to introduce myself. I'm Adolphus Burgesse. I do hope this unpleasantness won't deter you from continuing to deal with our firm."

To her father's credit, he stood, declined to return the gesture and said, "Unpleasantness doesn't begin to describe what has gone on here. The trouble seems to have started with a lack of confidentiality in your offices."

Burgesse peered over the top of his pince-nez. "Well, who was to know James Odlum would turn out to be ..."

Bea's father poked him in the chest. "You are expected to

employ people who can be trusted with confidential matters, not murderers and thieves."

Chastened, Burgesse mumbled an apology and regained his seat.

Bea linked arms with her father when he sat beside her, and patted his arm. "Living in the same house as Lucinda has evidently stiffened your backbone," she teased, not surprised when his face reddened.

Her father mumbled when Burgesse was summoned to testify and left the room.

"We'll be called one at a time," Barton explained. "That way, it's all independent testimony."

What little courage Bea had fled. "I wanted to go together," she told Roger. "I can't face this alone."

"We don't have much choice," he replied, meshing his fingers with hers.

The bank manager left next.

The knot in her stomach tightened further when first her father, then Roger were summoned to the courtroom.

ROGER FILLED his lungs and stepped through the heavy oak door held open for him by a clerk. The scene that greeted him was even more intimidating than he'd expected. Paneled with dark wood, the courtroom was much bigger than he'd anticipated. Against the far wall, a robed and bewigged judge presided from a seat raised high above the room itself.

At least ten wigged and gowned men occupied three rows of tall desks on the main floor of the courtroom. Roger assumed they were barristers and their clerks. Arthur, Burgesse, and the bank manager sat on a pew-like bench beside the witness box. The public gallery was packed. Seated in the front row, Lucinda nodded her encouragement. He glimpsed Mrs. Pickering near the back. Joss Pickering was probably in an alehouse somewhere. It was to be hoped Bea's aunt and uncle were not among the crowd.

The all-male jury sat in the jury box, every last one decked out in his Sunday best. They all looked prosperous, which Roger found reassuring.

His gaze finally settled on the man in the dock. Had he not known it was Peter Leigh, he wouldn't have recognized the gaunt wretch with the shaved head.

Led to the witness box, Roger placed his hand on the Bible and swore to tell the truth, the whole truth, and nothing but the truth.

A portly clerk asked his name and occupation. "Roger Sandiford," he replied, wishing he could spare Beatrice this ordeal. Neither of them had reason to be nervous, yet his breath caught in his throat when he added, "Master of Broadclough Mill in Bolton."

A tall, middle-aged barrister questioned him first about the murder and the subsequent investigation. He sounded so bored with the entire affair, Roger assumed he was the Crown counsel tasked with prosecuting Peter. Next came questions about his frantic ride to rescue Beatrice. Eyes fixed on Peter, Roger supplied details about the accident. He mentioned Peter threatening him with a pistol, but was careful to omit details of Beatrice's embarrassing predicament in the overturned carriage. Peter stared off into space as if the proceedings had nothing to do with him.

"I understand Mr. Leigh then stole your horse," the barrister said with great conviction.

"Yes," Roger replied, thinking that was the least of Peter's crimes, yet the barrister seemed keen to make the jury aware of it.

His next interrogator was a younger, pox-faced chap who put Roger in mind of his sister's husband. "Mortimer Featherstone, QC," he announced.

Roger knew the type. He couldn't resist bragging that he'd taken the silk and become a Queen's Counsel.

Looking over the top of his spectacles, Featherstone drawled, "It's alleged my client and the unfortunate Mr. Odlum committed murder on your premises after breaking in."

"Yes."

"Tell me, if you can, why they would choose your mill to break into."

Roger's throat tightened. He'd wondered the same thing and had no answer. "I don't know," he replied.

The barrister sat. "No further questions, M'Lud," he said, as he shuffled the papers on his desk.

Roger was dismissed. Perplexed, he took his place alongside his father-in-law as Sergeant Halliwell was brought into the courtroom.

Roger clamped his hands on his trembling knees while the policeman took the oath and identified himself. He was more nervous now he'd testified than before. Had he said the right things?

The prosecuting barrister led the sergeant through the stages of the investigation, from the discovery of the body to his conversation with Robbie Draper. He elicited information about the sergeant's meetings with the authorities in Preston, and the laying of subsequent charges of murder, theft, kidnapping, and horse theft against Peter Leigh.

Roger was impressed with Halliwell's professional demeanor. He never faltered once during the questioning, nor did he feel the need to consult his notebook. Nothing he said contradicted Roger's testimony. The jury couldn't fail to be impressed by him.

The policeman looked well pleased with himself by the time Peter's defense barrister rose to question him.

"Tell me, if you can, Sergeant, why Messrs. Odlum and Leigh would choose Sandiford's mill to break into."

Halliwell didn't blink. "Well, it's an interesting question. One I asked myself. I was perplexed, until the accused actually answered it for me."

Featherstone swallowed hard.

Complete silence reigned.

"Odlum had learned that Arthur Parker had inherited the mortgage on Broadclough Mill. He and Leigh conspired to make sure Mr. Sandiford's mill failed by damaging machinery there. Malcolm Pickering saw them, so they had to silence him. After that, they decided it was too risky to attack other mills. They surmised the late baron had hoarded his money and they concentrated on the plan to find and steal the cache. On top of that, forcing Miss Parker to marry Leigh would then make any male offspring the heir to a barony."

The sullen barrister muttered that he had no further questions.

Roger resisted the temptation to stand up and cheer.

Thaddeus Barton was sworn in next. Roger's thoughts went to Beatrice. She must be a nervous wreck after all this time and now she was alone—the last person left in the anteroom.

Barton described Leigh's capture with the stolen money in his possession. He corroborated everything Halliwell had said.

Barton's testimony over, the prosecutor addressed the judge. "M'Lud, there is one remaining witness, Mrs. Beatrice Sandiford, née Parker, but I'm sure Your Lordship will agree there is no need to subject a refined young lady to the scrutiny of the court. Surely we've heard enough without forcing Mrs. Sandiford to relive the horror she experienced."

"I agree," the judge replied gruffly. "Bailiff, inform Mrs.

Sandiford her testimony is no longer required. Members of the jury ..."

Roger didn't wait to listen to the instructions to the jury. He was confident they would fulfill their duty.

FIDDLING with the lace cuffs of her gown, Bea startled when the bailiff entered the anteroom. Dread lay like a lead ball in her stomach. She'd hoped she wouldn't have to face Peter, but the moment had finally arrived. Accepting the inevitable, she was about to rise when Roger burst through the door and took her into his arms. "The bailiff's here to tell you that your testimony isn't required," he exclaimed.

"Your testimony isn't required, Mrs. Sandiford," the bailiff repeated with a smile before exiting the anteroom.

"I don't understand," Bea said.

"The jury heard all they need to know from the other witnesses. The judge didn't want to subject a delicate young lady, such as yourself, to the ordeal of reliving the horror."

"Delicate! I must say I'm relieved, but I could have done it, you know."

"I know," he replied. "You may be from Dorset, but you've acquired some Lancashire brass."

"Which means?"

He kissed her cheek. "You're fearless, and you're mine."

"Let's go home and celebrate," she said, already aware of her husband's growing need of her.

"Amen to that," he replied.

Epilogue

P eter Leigh showed no reaction when the jury foreman read the verdict. He was found guilty on all counts and sentenced to be hanged.

Bea made it clear she didn't want to be informed when the sentence was carried out. As far as she was concerned, the sorry affair was over. Peter's death wouldn't bring Malcolm Pickering back to life, nor James Odlum for that matter.

She was pleased when her father broke all ties with Hardman, Burgesse, and Hilton after Roger recommended his own solicitors in Bolton.

They never heard from her aunt and uncle again.

Lucinda claimed to hate the cats that patrolled Belmont Grange. When kittens were born, she shipped them off to Sandiford Manor. Bea got used to having them underfoot and was only too happy to give them a good home.

Ventilation improved working conditions at Broadclough Mill. Roger invested in new machinery designed to weave calico, and was thus able to call some of his workforce back to work.

Marcus Halliwell's chest swelled as his superintendent pinned the medal for exemplary service to his uniform. He basked in the glow of handshakes and backslapping from fellow policemen who all seemed genuinely pleased he'd been promoted.

Later, having accepted a few too many congratulatory pints of ale at *The Nag's Head*, he filled his lungs and set off home, determined *Inspector* Halliwell wouldn't fail to solve his latest case—a gruesome murder at the Hippodrome Music Hall.

Historical Footnotes

COTTON COPS

You may be wondering why I gave this series the title COTTON COPS MYSTERIES. It's a play on the word for a spindle used in the cotton industry (cop), and of course, the word for a policeman. *http://revealinghistories.org.uk/why-was-cotton-so-important-in-north-west-england/objects/two-cotton-cops.html*

~

LANCASHIRE

Lancashire was the first industrial society in the world, the place where anything and everything was made, and where coal was mined. It was the birthplace of the factory system, and it needed a big population to operate the mines and factories. The first canal in the world was built in Lancashire, with more canals and railways following by the early 1830's. The workforce required was far bigger than the existing Lancashire population, and had to be imported from other counties, and from Ireland and Scotland. These men and women came from rural areas to live crammed together in the cities. Villages fast became towns.

Statistics show that Lancashire had a considerable crime rate compared with the rest of the country. In 1836, 2568 Lancastrians were convicted or tried for serious offenses.

Some towns formed their own police forces, but there was a growing demand for a county-wide force modeled on the London Metropolitan Police, brought into existence in 1829 by Sir Robert Peel. *https://en.wikipedia.org/wiki/Robert_Peel*

The Lancashire Constabulary was formed in 1840. *https://en.wikipedia.org/wiki/Lancashire_Constabulary*

~

RELIEF MEASURES during the *famine.*

In May 1862, £1500 (£180,000 in today's money) was sent to distressed areas of Lancashire and Cheshire by the Mansion House Fund. Benefactors from all over the United Kingdom, the Empire, and across the world raised money for the appeal. Mayors of the affected districts wrote letters to towns and cities all over the country. Between April 1862 and April 1863, £473,479 was collected and distributed (equivalent to £57.3 million).

~

THE COTTON FAMINE

https://en.wikipedia.org/wiki/Lancashire_Cotton_Famine

~

AMERICAN CIVIL WAR

https://www.theguardian.com/theguardian/from-the-

archive-blog/2013/feb/04/lincoln-oscars-manchester-cotton-abraham

Support for the embargo that resulted in the cotton famine.

∼

BOLTON

I chose Bolton as the setting for this story and the others in the series for one simple reason—I was born and went to school there! *https://en.wikipedia.org/wiki/Bolton*

You may be aware that I'm an amateur genealogist. Many of my nineteenth-century ancestors worked as spinners in the cotton mills.

About Anna & Acknowledgements

As an amateur genealogist (aka an addict of family tree research), I became obsessed with tracing my English roots back to the Norman Conquest in the 11th century.

This turned out to be a pipe dream, since I am not descended from the nobility and records were not kept for "common folks" until much later. Even then, early parish records are often indecipherable.

As a result, I began to write stories about a noble medieval family I conjured from my imagination. The Montbryces were born.

Like many people, I had an inner compulsion to write one good book. What was originally intended as that one book about my fictional family eventually became the 12-book series, *The Montbryce Legacy*.

In other words, writing superseded genealogy as my principal addiction, and I have since published more than sixty novels and novellas. Almost all are historical romances that feature Vikings, Highlanders, medieval knights, Elizabethan goldsmiths, or Regency aristocrats. You can find more details on my website https://annamarkland.com/.

I've lived most of my life in Canada, though I was born in the UK. An English grammar school education instilled in me a love of European history which continues to this day. While I may boast of being a proud Canadian, I'm still a Lancashire lass at heart.

Before becoming a full-time writer, I was an elementary

school teacher, a job I loved. I then worked as administrator for a world-wide disaster relief organization.

I love cats, although I haven't been able to bring myself to adopt another one since unexpectedly losing Topaz a few years ago.

I have few domestic skills. You'll notice most of my heroines hate sewing!

I try to follow three simple writing guidelines. I give my characters free rein to tell their story, which often turns out to be different from the original version in my head. I'm a firm believer in love at first sight. My protagonists may initially deny the attraction, but eventually, my heroes and heroines find their soulmates. It seems only natural then to include scenes of intimacy enjoyed by people who love each other deeply. I believe such intimacy is wholesome. Historical accuracy is important to me, although I have been known to tweak history when necessary. I write romance because I find happy endings very satisfying.

You can find me on all the usual social media platforms. On Facebook as Anna Markland and Anna Markland Novels, on Instagram as annamarkland, on X and Instagram as @annamarkland, and Pinterest and BookBub as Anna Markland. I also have a reader group on Facebook called Markland's Merrymakers, and new members are always welcome.

I'd be remiss if I didn't acknowledge the invaluable help of my beta readers, Maria McIntyre and Alison Pridie, and the creative genius of my cover designer, Dar at Wicked Smart Designs.

Also by Anna Markland

Cotton Cops Mystery Series

The Heart's Choice

Music Hall Queen

OTHER SERIES

Montbryce Legacy

Earls are Wild

FitzRam Family Dynasty

Clash of the Tartans

Montbryce Dynasty

The House of Pendray

Viking Roots Medieval

Von Wolfenberg Dynasty

The Caledonia Chronicles

Highland Whisky Kings

The UnDukes

Ruff Wooing

About the Author

Anna is a USA Today bestseller who has authored more than sixty award-winning and much-loved Medieval, Victorian, Viking, Highlander, Elizabethan and Regency historical romances. No matter the historical or geographic setting, many of her series recount the adventures of successive generations of one family, with emphasis on the importance of ancestry and honor. A detailed list with links can be found at https://www.annamarkland.com/

Getting the word out about her book is vital to its success. If you enjoy this book, please consider writing a review. Reviews help other readers find books.